The Cardinal, The Fat Boy & The Flamingo

Alice Kanaka

This book is a work of fiction. The events and characters portrayed are imaginary. Their resemblance, if any, to real-life counterparts is entirely coincidental. Actual places are used in a fictional context and this story is in no way portraying any real events, staff, internal workings, or management.

Table of Contents

Chapter 1

Riding into Las Vegas on her Fat Boy felt like sailing through an oven. Sam had traveled from Santo Milagro, New Mexico to meet up with *Torque*, a group of middle-aged bikers. She slowed and pulled into the Flamingo Hotel's parking garage. *I'm sure I've never seen this much pink. Ever. I can't wait to see it at night.* Her Harley's wide tires and reef blue trim stood out in the sea of red, black, and chrome. She grabbed her saddle bags and made her way inside.

The never-ending river of people and the black and white checkered tiles made Sam dizzy. The cold air in the lobby made the hair on her arms stand straight up, and she shivered violently as she approached the check-in desk.

The clerk smiled apologetically. "I'm sorry; it does take a little getting used to. How can I help you?"

"I have a reservation. Samantha Olivares."

She got checked in and received a key card for her newly renovated *Flamingo* room on the 25th floor of the *Habitat tower.*

Sam entered her room and looked around. Her gaze was drawn to the floor-to-ceiling window overlooking the strip. She set her saddle bags on the bed and walked to the window. *It's a beautiful view.* She turned and took a closer look at her room. It was tastefully decorated with gray and white; only the chairs and artwork were pink. *More pink, but at least it's just used as an accent.* She stripped off her dusty leathers and lightweight, long-sleeved shirt, briefly wondering about laundry services.

1

Then she stepped inside the shower, and all thought ceased. It felt so good to wash off the dust and sweat from the road.

As soon as she was clean, she called her friend, Cathy. "I'm here!"

"Great! Let's meet in the lobby, and I'll show you the big kids' pool. We can have a drink and relax."

Sam wondered about Cathy's terminology, but she was excited to see her, so she threw on her swimsuit and a robe and headed for the elevator.

The doors opened, and Cathy shouted, "I'm so glad you came!" She wrapped Sam in a big hug.

"Me too!"

"Once we get settled at the pool, you'll have to tell me what prompted your adventure."

When they arrived at the adults-only pool, Sam's head swiveled as she tried to take it all in. The first thing that hit her was the sound. The DJ had cranked up the music so it could be heard over the hoots and shrieks of the guests playing in the pool. Colorful swimsuits, beach balls, and floats vied for Sam's attention. She felt completely overwhelmed.

"Vegas really is somethin', isn't it," Cathy said, her brown eyes sparkling.

"Everything is bigger than life. It's amazing."

"Did you notice the waterfall?"

Sam marveled at the detail the hotel put into making the pool an island oasis.

"Let's get in the water and cool off. What'll you have to drink?"

"Something frozen sounds good. Strawberry margarita?"

"Ohh yeah." Cathy walked over to the bar and ordered two, then they took them and sat on the pool steps. "I see you've changed your hair."

Sam laughed and ran her hand through her spiky, turquoise hair. "I was getting tired of the red. This color matches my new bike."

2

"Really? What kind did you get?"

"It's a Harley Fat Boy. I love it! Lots of legroom."

Cathy eyed Sam's legs. "That's not one of my particular problems." She laughed. "I can't wait to see it."

They sipped their frozen drinks for a few minutes, watching the activity around the pool.

"I was surprised to hear from you." Cathy shifted on the step.

"I hope you don't mind."

"Not at all. It's just not too many people can drop everything to go on a road trip with a bunch of strangers."

"I felt a sudden need to get away. And I remembered you saying that I have to make my own adventure."

"Why did you need to get away?"

"A lot of things happened all at once, and I started questioning my place in the world, I guess." Cathy nodded as if she understood, but Sam knew she didn't.

"We all have dinner together if you want to meet everyone," Cathy said as she stood. "Tonight, we have a reservation at Carlos 'N Charlie's at seven. I know it's a little late, but it turns into a nightclub with dancing." Cathy's curls bobbed as she did a little shimmy, and Sam smiled. "Stay and splash around; maybe talk to that young man who's giving you the eye. I'll see you at seven." Cathy gave Sam a little nudge and a nod, then disappeared into the throng of people around the pool.

The man Cathy had mentioned sidled over from the bar with two cups. "Hi, I'm Cal. I thought you might like a refill." He handed her a cup. "The bartender said you had a frozen strawberry margarita." He winked.

She accepted the drink. "Thank you." Her stomach growled.

Cal smiled.

"Sorry. I completely forgot about lunch."

"The bar has food. Why don't we get you something to eat?"

Sam was taken aback. *This guy seems to have adopted me.*

3

"I'll just have some of this, then take a nap, I think." She raised her cup.

"Want some company?" Cal leered and ran his hand through his slicked-back red hair, showing off a bicep.

"Good one." Sam laughed.

Cal didn't seem to think it was funny. He scowled briefly. "Well, I'll see you tonight then."

"Tonight?"

"Yeah. I saw you talking to Cathy, so I assume she invited you to dinner."

"You know Cathy?"

"Of course. Her old man's the head honcho. We're tight."

"I guess I *will* see you at dinner then. Thanks for the drink." Sam stood to leave and could feel his eyes on her. *Great. I wonder why Cathy didn't warn me.* She left the pool, stopped at the food court, and took her lunch upstairs. Stretching out on the king-sized bed after she ate, she thought about her friends at home and her horse, Ghost. Then she started thinking about Jack but yanked her mind back from that precipice.

One minute she was awake, and the next, she was dreaming about flamingos dancing around a fire. They seemed to beckon her, and when she joined them, she turned into a flamingo too.

Waking with a start, she mulled over her dream and wondered if it was just the hotel theme. It was 6:45, so she had to hurry. *I didn't ask what kind of place it is. I hope it's not fancy.*

Cathy was sitting with Roy at the head of the table when Sam walked into Carlos 'N Charlie's. She wasn't sure what she thought about Sam joining them. She had enjoyed meeting her in New Mexico, but it had been just the girls, and Sam's open admiration and curiosity made her feel good. Here, though, Sam stuck out like a rare bird. She was tall and slender, naturally beautiful, and completely devoid of pretense. Even Roy was watching her.

"Is that your new friend?" he asked.

"Yes," she said as Sam arrived at the table. Cathy patted the chair next to her. "Sit here." Sam sat, and Cathy continued. "This is my husband, Roy." She leaned toward Roy. "Roy, this is Sam. She'll be joining us on our trip."

Roy extended his hand. "Nice to meet you, Sam. I hear you and Cathy met in Las Rodillas."

Sam leaned across Cathy and shook his hand. "We did. She made quite an impression on me."

"Welcome to *Torque*. We don't always live the high life. Lots of times we camp or stay at Airbnbs. But Vegas is special. Cathy and I met here."

"What a fun way to celebrate! I've never been to Vegas before. I guess maybe I should get some camping gear."

"We have extra for now. You can pick things up as you need them," Cathy said, bumping shoulders. "Oh! Here's Rachel! She's more your age."

She waved. "Rachel! Come meet my friend, Sam."

Rachel had a long, acne-scarred face and thin, blonde hair. She looked around, searching for Sam.

"Right here, dear." Cathy indicated.

"Oh! Sorry! Nice to meet you. May I?" Rachel pointed at the seat next to Sam.

"Of course!"

When Marcus came in and sat next to Roy, Cathy couldn't get an introduction in before Rachel excused herself and took the seat next to him. She leaned in and gave him an eyeful of cleavage before whispering something in his ear. He pushed her away and looked at Sam. "Hi. You're new," he said, smiling with white, even teeth.

"I was trying to introduce you." Cathy frowned.

"Why don't you wait until everyone gets here and introduce her once?" Rachel asked.

"Perhaps some of us would like to talk to her while we wait," Marcus countered.

Cathy sighed.

Two couples arrived, and Cathy said, "Lizzie! Dani! You remember Sam, don't you?"

"Of course!" Dani said, strutting over in her pink leather pants and stiletto heels. "It's great to see you again!" She hugged Sam. "This is my boyfriend, Pedro."

Pedro studied her with hooded, deep-set eyes and shook her hand.

Lizzie also walked over and offered a limp hand. "Will you be joining our road trip?"

Sam took her hand gently. "Yes. I hope you don't mind."

"As long as you get along with everyone, you're most welcome. This is my husband, Greg."

Greg grunted and gave a nod.

Everyone sat and stared at Cal as he made his entrance. He walked with a hitch in his stride, red hair slicked back, small paunch. He wore black slacks and a button-down shirt with a loosened tie.

Rachel rolled her eyes.

"I see you've all met my future wife," he said with a completely straight face.

Sam laughed, and everyone just stared at her until her eyes got a panicked look, then they all laughed. "You all got me good."

"I'll save you," Marcus said.

Rachel frowned.

God help us, Cathy thought.

"Sam, we've all eaten here several times. Do you have any idea what you'd like?" Roy asked.

Sam looked down the menu. "I'll try the shrimp tacos."

Cathy waved to the waiter and let him know they were ready to order, but when it was Dani's turn, she couldn't decide. "I don't know what I'm in the mood for." She leaned in and whispered in Pedro's ear.

"I need some food, babe. Why don't you get the chicken quesadilla? You liked that last time."

She licked her pouty lips. "I like other things too."

"Later."

"Maybe." She frowned.

They finished ordering, and Roy said something to Marcus that Cathy couldn't catch. However, when he stood and changed places with Greg, she knew he had business to discuss. She turned up the wattage of her smile. "So, Sam, what do you do for a living that lets you take off on a whim?"

"I'm a rancher, and I've never actually taken a vacation before. This is a first."

That didn't sound too interesting to Cathy, but the men at the table took an interest.

"So, you ride horses and lasso cows and stuff?" Cal asked.

"Sometimes, but I mostly make business decisions and keep the books. The ranch hands take care of most of the lassoing." Sam smiled.

"What kind of business decisions?" Pedro asked.

"How many head to buy or sell. How many calves we need. How much feed to buy. That sort of thing."

"That sounds fascinating, dear," Lizzie said.

Dani flipped her long, wavy hair. "No, it doesn't. No wonder you wanted to get away."

Cathy watched carefully. Sam's eyes widened a little at the blunt comment, but other than that, she gave no reaction.

"You are so rude," Rachel said. "Not everyone can spend all their time shopping."

Dani stuck out her tongue. "You should be the one on a ranch with a face like that," she mumbled.

Rachel's face turned red. "What's that supposed to mean?"

"You've seen it in the mirror. If it wasn't for your giant bazoongas, no man would even look at you."

"Ladies," Roy said quietly. "If you can't behave at the dinner table, perhaps you should excuse yourselves."

"I think I will. I shouldn't have to put up with her abuse. I'll be at the bar."

The waiter arrived with their food, and Rachel spoke with him before stalking off.

Sam excused herself for a moment, and Cathy saw her follow Rachel and sit with her. *She has a good heart.*

Sam sat across from Rachel. "Are you okay?"

"Just leave me alone. You don't know me."

Sam put her hand on Rachel's. "That's true. But I know when someone is being mean. And I know it hurts when I'm on the receiving end."

"Has anyone ever said something like that to you?"

"I've been made fun of because of my height and my hair and my lack of girliness. I know what it feels like."

"I know I'm not beautiful." Rachel sighed. "But I do the best I can with what I have."

Sam looked her in the eye. "You may have features you don't like. Everyone does. But you, as a total package, are beautiful. When you walk into a room, men's heads swivel. Whatever Dani said was probably motivated by jealousy."

"Why would she be jealous of me?"

"Pedro has a roving eye, and Dani has her own insecurities. I know that doesn't make her words any less painful, but I've known people like her. They say the most painful thing they can think of when they feel attacked and sometimes don't even remember they said it later. My best friend's mother was like that."

Rachel's eyes glistened. "Thanks, Sam. That helps a little."

"Would you like me to bring my dinner over here and eat with you?"

"No, go ahead and join the others. I'll see you on the dance floor."

Sam stood and hugged her briefly before rejoining the dinner party.

Cathy saw Sam returning and shushed everyone.

Sam sat and looked at her plate. "Did someone steal one of my tacos?"

Marcus raised his hand slowly, with a sheepish smile. "It was getting cold. I thought one of us should enjoy it."

Sam playfully whacked his shoulder with the back of her hand. "I trusted you."

"Never trust a handsome man," Cathy said.

"The rest of us are ready to order dessert," Lizzie said.

"Don't worry about me." Sam grinned. "The frozen margaritas are dessert enough."

Dani mumbled, "Just one probably has a thousand calories."

Sam raised an eyebrow but kept her smile.

"That is why we have to hit the dance floor after dinner," Cathy said with a shimmy.

They finished their meal with equanimity, then moved into the bar area.

Roy sat with Sam while she finished her meal, and together they watched the women walk through the crowd. Cathy was the epitome of a 60s flower child, now in her 50s. She was vivacious, with colorful, flowing clothes. Lizzie reminded Sam of a young Audrey Hepburn, only not so young. Dani played the role of sex kitten.

She saw Dani speak to Rachel with her head down and offer her a hug. All seemed to be forgiven, but Sam wondered.

Roy cleared his throat. "We're an interesting group, don't you think?"

"Yes, actually. You're all so different, yet everyone seems to get along... mostly."

He leaned forward. "What are you *really* doing here? Are you a cop?"

Sam's eyes widened, and she gaped. "No! Is that what you think? That I have some sinister motive for joining you?"

"You have to admit, it seems a little suspicious."

Sam shrugged. "I'll tell you the whole story if you need me to."

"Please."

She paused and bit her lip. "My father died a year and a half ago, and it left me feeling very alone. Then, in early Spring, a cousin I had forgotten about showed up."

Roy nodded, watching her intently. "How do you forget you have a cousin?"

Sam shrugged. "Our fathers had a disagreement when we were very young. I hadn't seen nor heard of him since I was five."

"I see."

"Anyway, after he arrived, there were two murders, two attempted murders, and a kidnapping. We both got involved. Life was hectic and busy. I had friends and a relative and lots of adventure."

Roy's eyebrows went up. "You enjoyed the murder investigation? How did you get involved if you're not a cop?"

"My friends were getting hurt, and I got kidnapped. I didn't enjoy that. I don't know. I enjoyed collaborating and hanging out with my cousin. In our downtime, we went camping, had pool parties, and had friends over."

"Your life was social and full."

"Then it was all over." Sam sighed. My cousin went home, a friend was dead, and I found out another friend had had an affair with my father for years. I was suddenly lonely and bored."

Roy got a faraway look in his eyes. "I felt that way when I returned from my tour of duty. Being deployed was hell, but I missed the camaraderie and sense of purpose when I came home. I couldn't settle down, so I started this group."

"So maybe you understand. I just felt like I needed to get away. Anywhere. Then I remembered Cathy. She told me I had to make my own adventures, that no one else would make them for me. I saw her 'Have a nice day' card on my desk and called her. That's all."

"That's all? Sounds like you've been through it. Where is your cousin now?"

"He's back in Albuquerque."

Roy gave her a little smile, but his eyes looked sad. "I'm sorry for raking all that up, but I like to know what kind of people my friends are."

"I understand. I think I would feel the same way."

"If you're done there, perhaps we should join the others."

Sam smiled. "I'm done."

They stood and made their way to the bar. Pedro and Dani were dancing, Marcus was having a discussion with the bartender, and Cal was hitting on every woman he could find. Rachel, looking recovered, asked Roy to dance.

Cathy got a dangerous glint in her eye. She watched the two of them on the dance floor, her brows furrowed. Then she turned and glared at Sam. "What were you and Roy talking about for so long?"

"He thought I was a cop. I had to explain why I joined you guys."

Cathy immediately relaxed and laughed. "I'm going to head upstairs. Want to go shopping tomorrow?"

"That sounds fun. We could have lunch together while we're out."

"Great! Let's meet in the lobby around ten."

Cathy said goodnight and disappeared into the crowd. Sam stayed for a while and danced until Cal set his sights on her. She saw him heading in her direction, so she went to the bar where Marcus was still talking to the bartender. He looked slightly annoyed at her interruption, but the bartender winked at him and walked away.

"You said you'd protect me," Sam said with pleading eyes. "Just dance me toward the exit, so I can escape. Please?"

Marcus looked over her shoulder at Cal and smiled. "Let's make it look good." He took her hand and led her onto the dance floor, pulling her uncomfortably close. His hands were in places they shouldn't have been, and he put his lips near her ear.

"I would be alarmed if I hadn't seen how you looked at that guy behind the bar."

"It's all for show. I would be alarmed if I thought you couldn't keep a secret."

"Partners in crime." She grinned.

"My uncle can't know."

"Who's your uncle?"

"Another secret."

"Okay. Cal has moved on to another target. Dance me toward the entrance, and I'll make my escape."

He saw Cal watching them, so he kissed her.

"I am now jealous of the bartender. You just set my socks on fire."

"Yeah, that was a good one." He grinned at her. "I think Cal got the message."

"Thank you, my hot, unavailable hero." Sam walked quickly out of the restaurant and up to her room. It wasn't late, but she felt exhausted. She lay down for a minute and didn't wake until morning.

Chapter 2

Cathy quickly left the Cosmopolitan suite where she and Roy were staying. When she turned toward the elevators, she almost ran into Lizzie exiting the room next door. "Oh! Excuse me. I'm afraid Roy's been rushing me because he has some mysterious meeting." Lizzie blushed slightly, and Cathy knew she had heard at least part of her conversation with Roy. They stepped onto the elevator. "Would you like to join Sam and I? We're going shopping."

"That's nice of you, but I'm supposed to meet Greg after his golf game."

Cathy smiled. "You two are such a great couple." The elevator doors opened, and they stepped out.

"It's work sometimes," Lizzie said, not quite meeting Cathy's gaze. "See you at dinner."

Cathy watched Lizzie walk toward the bar, then hurried to meet Sam in the lobby.

Sam was relieved when Cathy arrived because Cal was hovering and wouldn't take *no* for an answer.

"Cal! Will you be joining our shopping trip?" Cathy asked as she approached Sam.

He frowned. "You couldn't pay me enough."

"We'll see you at dinner then. Let's get a move on, Sam."

They walked out of the hotel, and Sam said, "Thank God for that."

Cathy looked at Sam and raised her eyebrows. "What happened?"

"He's just such a pest." Sam shrugged. "He won't leave me alone."

"Oh, I know, dear. He's like that with all the single ladies… except Rachel. He doesn't like her for some reason."

"Hm. Maybe I should ask her what her secret is."

Cathy ignored her comment. "I thought we could walk down the Linq Promenade to the *High Roller*." Cathy pointed to a giant Ferris wheel.

"That sounds great!" Sam looked around at the crowd and shuddered a little, but as they walked, she found herself focusing on the little things. Sam remembered taking a hike with Jack in the desert and showing him all the little details that would be missed on horseback. She noticed couples and families from many different cultures, listening to their languages and noticing different clothing styles.

Sam heard music everywhere: blaring from stores, speakers, and boom boxes, competing for people's attention from opposite corners. Shoppers and pedestrians spoke loudly to be heard over the music.

So much noise. I wonder if I'll be deaf by the time I get home.

They looked in the myriad shops, beginning with the Welcome to Las Vegas store. "I'm not much of a shopper," Sam said, "but I would like to find some souvenirs for my friends back home."

Cathy nodded. "Just look around, and something is bound to catch your eye. Sometimes I pick up little trinkets too."

Sam wandered up and down aisles spilling over with cheap, high-priced, and often gaudy items that no one would ever use. She picked out some key chains, socks, and a couple of t-shirts as she browsed. She wasn't entirely pleased with her purchases, but space was an issue.

She and Cathy stopped to watch a group of street performers outside the store.

Five men performed a combination of hip hop and gymnastics while engaging the crowd and pulling them into the performance. The group was funny and creative, a big hit. Sam would have stayed longer to watch, but Cathy reminded her of the time.

They walked on until Sam stopped in her tracks and gawked at the one store that could make her a shopper. As she gazed at the large Harley Davidson logo and the plate glass windows, she thought she might have heard angels sing if it weren't for all the competing sounds. "Cathy! We have to go in there!" She grabbed Cathy's hand and pulled her inside, then just stood and let the rows of cool gear and the smell of leather wash over her. "This is nothing like the store in Las Rodillas."

Sam was fascinated by all the gear and accessories. She found herself buying much more than she had intended. Then, burdened down with shopping bags, Cathy led her to a shop that sold cupcakes, and they sat on the edge of a fountain to rest.

"What did you get?" Cathy asked, eyeing Sam's bags.

Sam groaned. "What didn't I get? Shopping in Las Rodillas is sparse. I got carried away. Custom parts, souvenirs, clothes, they had everything!"

Cathy laughed. "I get like that in yarn shops."

"What? Why?"

"I knit. I love to make colorful things."

"That makes sense. Your love of color is evident." Sam smiled.

Suddenly, Cathy stood. "Do you want to eat first or take a ride?"

Sam looked up and was surprised at how close they were to the *High Roller*. "Let's ride first. I'm excited to see the view, and we did have that cupcake."

The observation wheel seemed to grow exponentially the closer they got. Sam was rubbernecking by the time they got in line. Instead of small seats for two, large enclosed 'cabs' each held up to forty people. Luckily, their cab wasn't too full, and they were able to get a good view.

Cathy pointed out the sights as they sailed slowly through the sky. She was surprised at how fun and easy it was to hang out with Sam. She was much younger but curious about her surroundings and very low maintenance. *I hope the others are wrong and she doesn't have an agenda. I hope she doesn't get hurt. She seems like she can hold her own.*

Once their ride was over, Sam said, "That was incredible. I had no idea how much is packed into this area. It would take weeks, maybe months, to see it all."

Cathy nodded. "We've been here dozens of times, and I haven't seen a fraction of it."

Sam's stomach growled, and Cathy laughed. "I guess you're hungry. What should we eat?"

"I don't know. Do you have a favorite?"

"You might think it's silly, but I just love In 'N Out."

"I've never eaten there."

"Then, follow me. You're in for a treat!"

They walked back down the promenade in silence until the big red sign with the yellow arrow came into view. "Behold," Cathy said, "the mecca of burgers."

"All this hype, and I'm starting to get pretty excited."

"And so you should. Let's go in and get some."

They placed their orders for cheeseburgers, animal fries, and shakes. Cathy ordered an extra burger for Roy. "He loves these too." She smiled. When a table opened, Cathy sent Sam to claim it. "Animal fries definitely require a table."

She could tell Sam didn't understand what she meant until she took the food to the table and unloaded the bags. Sam opened the box and grabbed her fork. "Mmm," she said through a mouthful of food. "I might be willing to move here just for these fries."

Cathy smiled as she opened her own box. "I always eat them first, or they get soggy."

When they were done with lunch, they headed back to the hotel with Roy's burger. "Come on up with me and see our suite. It's so cute.

16

We got it because sometimes we like to entertain instead of going out."

"Is it very pink?"

"You could say that." Cathy laughed.

"Thank you so much for today," Sam said as they entered the elevator. "I had a great time."

"I did too."

The elevator dinged, and the doors opened. Sam and Cathy stepped out into a world of chaos.

Chapter 3

Crime scene tape blocked off one of the rooms, and officers and techs milled around. Cathy's eyes widened, and she began to shake, dropping her food bag. "That's our room," she whispered. "Roy?" She rushed up to an officer. "What's going on? I need to get inside."

"I'm sorry, ma'am, this is a crime scene. Can I have your name, please?"

"This is my room." Cathy's voice grew in intensity and pitch. "What happened? Is my husband okay?"

Sam picked up the bag and approached Cathy. She put her hand on Cathy's arm and gave the officer a small smile. "Is there someone who can talk to her about what happened, officer?"

"Yes. If you two could wait over by the elevators, I'll get the detective in charge."

Sam tried her best to stay calm for Cathy, but her heart was beating hard.

The officer strode over to the detective in charge. "Sir, two ladies showed up. One says this is her room, and she's asking about her husband. The other asked if there's someone they could talk to."

The detective looked toward the elevators, where the officer was pointing. One of the ladies was middle-aged, with short, curly hair and a round, cheerful-looking face. She didn't look very cheerful at the moment. The other woman was young, perhaps his age. She was about his height too. Tall and thin with a petite face and short blue hair. "Thank you. I'll take care of it."

He approached them confidently, extending his hand. Sam shook his hand, but Cathy stared at him with eyes like saucers. "I'm Detective Thomas Cork. May I have your names, please?"

"I'm Samantha Olivares, and this is my friend, Cathy Williams. That's her room. Could you tell us what has happened?"

I should get her to identify the body before her friend tries to interfere. "In just a moment. Could you come with me, Mrs. Williams?"

Cathy nodded dumbly and allowed the detective to lead her into the room while Sam waited in the hall.

Tom looked back at Sam and saw her slide down the wall to sit on her heels. He turned to Cathy. "I know this is difficult, but I need your help." They entered the suite and passed between the dining and living areas. As they rounded the couch, a body lay outlined on the floor, surrounded by crime scene analysts and a photographer. Cathy trembled as they approached the body. "Can you identify this man?"

Cathy gasped and lunged forward. "Roy!"

Tom stopped her from touching the body and gently asked, "Is this your husband?"

"Y-yes. R-roy Williams." Tears coursed down her face. "What happened? Who did this?"

"I don't know yet, but I'll find out. I'm very sorry for your loss."

"We argued this morning. I brought him In 'N Out to make up. Now I'll never be able to say I'm sorry." She slumped to the floor, sobbing.

"Harve! Give me a hand, please!"

The two detectives helped Cathy back to the hallway where Sam was waiting.

"Ms..."

"Olivares."

"Can Mrs. Williams stay with you until we can arrange for another room?"

"Of course! Can she have her things?"

"Not quite yet. I'll have someone bring them when we're finished here. Could I have your room number, please?"

"2506."

"Thank you." He helped Sam move Cathy toward the elevator.

"I'm so sorry, Cathy. Let's get you to my room so you can relax."
Cathy clutched at Sam and spoke incoherently.

"I know," Sam said gently, even though she didn't understand what Cathy was saying. She shifted her shoulder under Cathy's arm so she could help her onto the elevator, and Tom backed up as the doors opened.

"I'm sorry again, Mrs. Williams. We'll get you your things as soon as possible." He nodded to Sam and tried to memorize her face as the doors closed, then turned and walked back to the Williams' hotel room.

He walked around, mumbling to himself and taking notes. "Air conditioning. Why is it so cold in here?" He noted two glasses sitting on the coffee table but no beverage. *Did he have a drink with someone? If so, where's the bottle?* He stepped into the bedroom. Although the bed hadn't been made, the room was very neat and tidy. The dining area looked oddly cheerful, with neon pink cushions on the chairs. Mr. Williams lay prone in the sitting area, with two bullet holes in his chest. "No weapon. No struggle. Broken watch. Dirt?" His brow furrowed. "Harve. Where's the housekeeper? I have some questions."

"She's in the manager's office, sir."

"Thank you. I'll be back."

Tom made his way to the manager's office and pulled out his badge, showing it to a woman sitting next to the manager's desk. "I'm Detective Thomas Cork. Are you Gladys Pepper?"

She nodded.

He looked toward the manager. "Thank you for your cooperation. Could we use your office for a private interview?"

"Oh, of course." She gathered her things. "I'll just be in the office next door if you need me."

"Thank you."

Tom stepped to the side as she was leaving and took note of Gladys. Thirties, eyes puffy from crying, and her makeup irreparably smeared. As the manager quietly closed the door behind her, he couldn't help wondering why Gladys was so upset. Surely this wasn't her first body. It was Las Vegas, after all. "This must have been a terrible shock. Are you able to answer some questions?"

"You can't think I did it! I didn't even know him." Her lip quivered, and her eyes began to well up.

Tom raised a single brow and leaned against the desk. Perhaps his hunch had been right. "I just want to hear what happened, what you saw, so we can catch whoever did this."

Gladys let out a breath she'd been holding and slumped a little. "I'll tell you."

"Start at the beginning."

"I knocked and then unlocked the door with my key card."

"So, the door was closed and locked?"

"They lock automatically when they close. So, I went in with my cart and called out that I was there, but there was no answer."

"Did you notice anything odd?"

"The drapes were closed, and it was very cold."

Tom's brow furrowed. "How cold?"

"I got goose pimples. It was like a refrigerator. I went over to turn down the A/C, and I tripped over the body." Gladys trembled. "It was pretty dark in there, but when I saw someone was on the floor, I turned on the light. I thought maybe the person had passed out. It happens quite a bit... Then I saw the blood, and I started to scream. I couldn't seem to stop. Someone must have called security because the next thing I knew, someone was helping me to my feet and guiding me out of the room."

"You weren't on your feet?"

"I don't remember that part too well."

"Do you know the security person?"

"No. I think he was wearing camo gear. I feel a little mixed up about that."

"What's the next thing you remember?"

"He left me in the hall and went back inside. Then he waited with me until the police came. He must have called from the room?"

Tom rubbed his chin. "No cell phone?" he mumbled. "The manager came to get you after the police came?"

Gladys nodded.

"And the security man?"

"I don't know where he went."

"Thank you very much. Here's my card. Please let me know if you remember anything else."

"Sir?" She looked up at him. "When we were in the hall, there was a person peeking through a crack in the door of the next room. I think the man might have gone there after the police came."

"Which side?"

"The left."

"Do you remember anything about what he looked like? Other than the camo?"

Gladys closed her eyes. "I think... he had gray hair. And a mustache. He looked more like a soldier than security."

"Wonderful. You have been a great help." Tom smiled.

She smiled back tentatively and sniffed.

"Goodbye for now and thank you."

Gladys nodded but stayed where she was when he left. Tom poked his head into the office next door and thanked the manager before heading back upstairs.

Chapter 4

Sam and Cathy were sitting at the small table in Sam's room having coffee when someone knocked on the door. Sam hurried over and opened it. "Hello, detective."

"Hello. This is Detective Harvey Brother."

Harvey stuck out his hand to shake Sam's and smiled. "Pleased to meet you."

"Nice to meet you, too. Come on in."

Sam closed the door behind them and ushered them toward the partially covered windows. The mood was somber, and yet Tom felt energy radiating from Sam.

"Roy said to never invite a policeman in," Cathy slurred.

Tom turned to Cathy, who had apparently been drinking something other than coffee. "I know this is a difficult time, Mrs. Williams, but I need to ask some preliminary questions to get an idea of what we're looking at."

Cathy looked at him with tired, red eyes. "What do you need to know?"

"First, was it just the three of you traveling together?"

"No, there are ten of us." Cathy doubled over with her arms crossed. "Nine now." She rocked back and forth a few times.

"Ten? Family reunion?"

"We're a motorcycle club. *Torque*. We've been traveling across the southern states."

"Could I ask you to wait outside, Ms... Olivares?"

Sam stood. "Yes, of course." She left the room with a backward glance at Cathy.

Tom sat at the table with Cathy, and Harvey pulled out his notebook and perched on the edge of the bed.

"Where do you consider home?" Tom continued once the door had closed.

"We lived in Florida, but we sold our house and took to the road. Roy had a hard time settling down after his last deployment."

"He was a vet?"

"Yes. Command Sergeant Major out of AMSA in Florida."

"How long ago did you sell your house?"

"About two years."

"Were you happy about your new lifestyle?"

Her glance flicked from one man to the other. "Mostly." *Why are they asking that? Am I a suspect?*

Tom rubbed his chin. "Did the others join you right away?"

"No. Lizzie and Greg are old friends. They joined us first."

"Last name?"

"Scott." Cathy glanced at Harvey, who was scribbling furiously. "Do I need a lawyer?"

"I don't know. I'm just trying to figure out who knew you and your husband and their relationships to you. As a starting place. If I don't assume that the murderer is someone close to you, the entire city of Las Vegas and all of the guests at the Flamingo will be suspects. I'm gathering background information."

"Oh." Cathy processed that for a moment. "Alright. I want to help. The next to join was Greg's friend, Pedro, and his girlfriend, Dani."

"Please include last names if you know them."

"Pedro Nunez and Danielle Golden."

"Who was next?"

"Pedro's friend Cal Lenox, then a loner named Rachel Simon, then Marcus Rhodes. I think he might be related to Roy. Sam, Samantha Olivares, just joined us yesterday."

"And how do you know her?"

"I met her when we passed through New Mexico.

She called out of the blue and asked if she could join us."

Harvey looked up from his notebook. "So, you don't really know her?"

"Not very well. No."

Tom leaned forward a little. "What reason did she give for joining you?"

"Look, even if her arrival seems suspicious, she couldn't have done it because she was with me all morning. Her reason is personal and irrelevant."

"You said you argued with Roy this morning. What was that about?"

Cathy put her head in her hands. "He wanted me to hurry and leave because he had some business meeting. I got mad. It was stupid, and I wish I had told him I loved him before I left." Her shoulders began to quake.

"I'm sure he knew." Tom paused. "What kind of business was Roy conducting?"

Cathy shrugged. "I don't know, but Greg might. He was very secretive about it."

"What time did you leave?"

Cathy looked at him sharply.

"Sorry, I'm just letting them loose as I think of them."

"I'm not sure. I was supposed to meet Sam at ten, so before that."

"Did you see anyone else?"

"No. Well, Cal was talking to Sam when I got to the lobby."

"Did your husband own a gun?"

Cathy shifted uncomfortably in her chair. "Yes."

"Do you know where he kept it?"

"He always had it with him."

"Do you know what kind it was?"

"No."

"Were the drapes closed when you left?"

Cathy shook her head.

25

"One last question. Do you usually keep your room very cold?"

"A little. I sometimes get hot flashes."

Tom nodded. "Thank you for helping us. The hotel manager has agreed to get you a different room. Detective Brother will take you down to the front desk while I speak with Ms. Olivares."

Tom and Harvey both stood.

"Thank you, detective." Cathy sniffed and rose shakily from her chair. "Please find the person who did this."

Harvey took her elbow and helped her to the door, nodding to Sam that it was her turn.

Tom turned as Sam approached. She was much younger than Cathy and appeared calm. He shook her hand and gestured for her to sit. "Thank you for waiting."

Sam sat quietly and almost imperceptibly nodded with a small smile.

"Mrs. Williams told me that you just arrived yesterday."

"Yes."

"How did you meet?"

Sam smiled, thinking back. "I was in a diner in New Mexico with my cousin and a local policeman when I saw Cathy and her friends for the first time. They were so vivacious and full of energy. I guess I was staring. Cathy came over and asked if I had a problem with them." Sam laughed at the memory. "The next thing I knew, she was buying me a beer and introducing me to her friends."

Tom tilted his head. "What made you decide to join them?"

"Roy asked me the same thing last night after dinner."

"You had dinner with him?"

"We *all* had dinner together, but there was a small argument between two of the women. I followed the one who left to make sure she was okay, so I finished eating last. Roy stayed at the table to find out why I'm here. He thought I might be a police officer." She chuckled.

"But you're not." He eyed her closely.

"Do I look like a cop?"

"We come in all sorts of packages."

"True. Well, I'm not." Sam shrugged. "I've just had a rough year and wanted to get away."

"You're from New Mexico?"

"Yes. A small town called Santo Milagro."

"Your occupation?"

"Rancher."

"Marital status?"

"Single. You?"

He looked up from his notes, surprised. "Single." Then he stared at her and smiled. "Don't try to distract me."

"I was just curious."

"Who were the two ladies who argued last night?"

"Dani and Rachel. Rachel told Dani she was rude, then Dani made some ugly, personal insults. Roy told them if they couldn't behave at the table, then maybe they should excuse themselves."

Tom leaned forward. "Yesterday was the first time you met them?"

"I met Lizzie and Dani at the diner when I met Cathy."

"Anything else of note from the dinner party?"

Sam's eyes went up as she thought back to the previous night. "I got general first impressions of everyone. At one point, Roy asked Marcus to switch places with Greg. Cathy said they were probably discussing business. Cal is kind of creepy toward women."

"What time did you meet Cathy this morning?"

"At ten."

"Where'd you go?"

"She took me down the Linq Promenade to the *High Roller*, then we had lunch."

"And you were together the whole time you were out?"

"Yes, except when we used the restroom or tried something on."

Tom leaned back and crossed his right ankle over his left knee. "You said you were at a diner with your cousin and a policeman when you met her. Tell me about them."

Sam raised her eyebrows. "My cousin is the Chief Medical Examiner for New Mexico."

"Name?"

"Jack Olivares."

"And the policeman?"

"Sergeant Dennis Mickelson from Santo Milagro."

"And why were the three of you together?"

"We're friends, but we were also working on a double homicide."

The ankle came down with a thump. "I thought you weren't a police officer."

"I was volunteering as a local consultant."

Tom frowned a little.

"Santo Milagro is very small."

"How did you get to Vegas?"

"I rode a motorcycle."

"By yourself?"

"Yes." Sam's eyes twinkled.

"Where is it now?"

"In the parking garage."

"Will you show me?"

"Sure. But you're gonna be jealous." Sam grinned.

The blast of heat outside hit him like a furnace. *I'll never get used to this.* When they got to Sam's parking spot, she indicated her bike, and he might have drooled a little. "You're right; I'm a little jealous." He ran his hand along the beautiful lines of her Fat Boy. "It matches your hair."

"Do you want to ride?"

Tom's pulse went up a notch. "Not just now, but I might take you up on it when I close this case."

"No riding the suspect's bike?"

"Something like that." He saw her eyes follow his hand as he gently ran it along the seat of the bike. *What is wrong with me?* He snatched his hand away from the motorcycle.

"It's still new, so I might have had a panic attack letting someone else ride it anyway." Her eyes twinkled, and he knew she was only half joking.

"Your ranch must be doing very well."

"It's a large ranch, but I also inherited some money from my uncle. This was my birthday present to myself."

Tom smiled. "It's a great present. I've got one more question, then I'll stop taking up your time."

She looked at him expectantly.

"If you had to take a guess, who do you think might have killed Roy?"

Sam's eyebrows furrowed. "I really have no idea. He seemed like such a nice man, but I only saw him during that one dinner. I would probably start by interviewing Greg. He knew him best, I think, and he knows all the others."

Tom took one last look at Sam's Fat Boy. "May I walk you back inside?"

Sam nodded, and they walked back into the lobby in silence. He shook her hand again and thanked her. Her energy was palpable, and he was reluctant to let go. "Please give me a call if you think of anything else." He gave her his card.

"I will. Thank you."

He watched her walk to the elevators, where she turned and gave him a little wave as she stepped inside. Then, he approached the front desk and asked to speak with someone in security. He made an appointment to review the security footage and requested the room numbers for each person on his list.

Chapter 5

While he waited for his appointment with the head of security, Tom sat in one of the hotel's empty conference rooms and took out his phone. He called the Santo Milagro sheriff's station and asked to speak with Sergeant Mickelson.

"Hello. This is Mick."

"Hello. This is Detective Cork calling from the Las Vegas Police Department. I understand you had a civilian consultant by the name of Samantha Olivares helping with a case earlier this year."

"Yes. We've missed her. Will you be sending her home soon?" Mick laughed, and Tom's shoulders relaxed a little.

"Do you remember having lunch with her when she met a group of motorcycle riders?"

"I had almost forgotten that. We were at Mary's diner in Las Rodillas with Jack. They were an odd bunch, but Sam seemed very taken with one of the gals. We had to practically drag her away. Can you tell me what this is about? Does Sam need help?"

"Ms. Olivares is fine. I'm just checking on some bona fides. Thank you very much for your assistance."

"You're welcome. What did you say your name was again?"

"Thomas Cork. You can call and verify," Tom said with a smile.

"Thank you, Detective. You take care of our Sam. She's special."

Tom looked at his phone as he disconnected. *Yes, Santo Milagro is a small town, but how many cops would say that about anyone?*

He dialed the medical examiner's office in New Mexico next and asked for Jack Olivares.

Jack came on the line, and Tom once again introduced himself.

"How can I help you, Detective?"

"I understand that you were in Santo Milagro earlier this year, working on a double homicide with Sergeant Mickelson."

"Yes, that's correct."

"And you were assisted by your cousin, Samantha Olivares?"

"Yes. Is she okay?"

"She is fine. Do you recall having lunch when she met a group of motorcycle riders?"

Jack chuckled. "She's very good at making friends. I miss her. Are you sure she's okay?"

"Yes. I'm just verifying statements. What is her occupation?"

"She's a rancher."

"Does she travel often?"

"No. I don't think she's gone anywhere since university. Until now."

"Do you know why she came to Vegas?"

"Yes, I think so."

"Could you tell me?"

"It's pretty personal, so you should probably ask her."

"Okay. Well, thank you for your time."

"I'm glad you called. You've reminded me that I should call her. It's been too long."

Tom nodded, even though Jack couldn't see him. He disconnected and stared at the phone again. He felt relieved that she checked out and he could tentatively take her off the suspect's list but worried about his motivation. *I don't know what's the matter with me. I've never been this irrational about a suspect... or someone who's even remotely involved in a case... or anyone, if I'm honest.* He shook his head as if to remove the cobwebs and went in search of Harvey.

Harvey was sitting patiently in the lobby when Tom found him. "We have an appointment with security, then we'll head back upstairs.

Harvey, a junior detective, had started his training with an older detective who didn't want any input. He was often silent and reticent about leading interviews or giving his opinion. Tom sometimes forgot he was there. "Do you have any thoughts after spending time with Mrs. Williams?"

Harvey gave the impression of physical withdrawal. Tom thought he looked like he somehow shrunk inward. *I wonder how he does that.* He waited patiently.

Harvey blushed a little under Tom's scrutiny. "I think she might have done it, sir."

"And why is that?"

"Sometimes she gets distracted and seems to forget he's even dead."

"Not everyone reacts the same way to loss. Is there any evidence that points to her?"

They had reached security, but Tom stopped in the hallway to let Harvey finish his assessment.

"Well, sir, she shared the room, and we only have her word that he was alive when she left. He trusted her, and she had access to his gun."

"It's a possibility." Tom nodded. "Let's keep open minds while we interview the others, though."

Harvey straightened his spine a little.

Tom knocked, and James Parker, head of security, opened the door. "Come on in," he boomed.

They followed him to a table, set up with a computer and headphones. "Have a seat. Most of the cameras don't have sound because, with all of the noise, we can't usually hear any conversation anyway. I have footage from all of the relevant cameras from ten to one. Take your time."

"Thank you very much. I appreciate it."

Tom and Harvey sat for several hours looking through the footage. Harvey dozed off at one point, and Tom almost missed someone visiting Roy's room when he looked down at his notes.

32

In fact, two people had visited his room, which cleared Cathy as a suspect.

Tom roused Harvey and said, "Okay, sleepyhead, let's go interview the Scotts."

Harvey was embarrassed and fell over himself, apologizing.

"I know it's mind-numbing work but remember that our goal is to catch a killer."

They rode the elevator to the 28th floor. Crime scene tape still surrounded the Williams' room. Tom turned toward room 2815 and knocked. He could hear voices inside, but no one came to the door. He knocked again and was finally rewarded with an answer.

Greg, dressed all in camouflage, opened the door a crack. "Who are you?"

"I'm Detective Thomas Cork of the LVPD, and this is Detective Harvey Brother."

"Come in. Come in. After what happened earlier, we can't be too careful." He let the detectives in and closed the door, leading them into the sitting area. "Please, have a seat."

Tom looked around. The room was almost identical to the room next door, except there were personal items lying around. Reading glasses and a newspaper sat on the coffee table. Snacks and liquor bottles perched on the counter in the dining room. Two pairs of shoes lay haphazardly by the door.

"What happened earlier?"

Greg leaned in and whispered, "the murder."

"How do you know about that?" Tom raised an eyebrow.

"I'm the one who called it in."

"Can you describe your movements for us?"

"Of course." Greg's chest puffed out as he sat straighter. "The wife and I got back from the bar, and we heard screaming. It sounded like someone was being attacked. I went to get my gun, but it's missing. Anyway, I grabbed a knife and told Lizzie to lock the door behind me. I crept into the hall, and Roy's door was open.

It was dark in there, and the maid was standing between the dining and living areas, screaming her head off. I led her out of the room and went back to see what the problem was. When I went to open the curtains, I saw Roy. I took his pulse and called 911, then went back out to let Lizzie know and to wait with the maid."

Tom looked at Harvey, who was scribbling away. *The maid said she turned on the lights before she saw the body. Why did Greg say it was dark?* "Did you notice anything strange about the room?"

Greg frowned. "The room was neat, but it was freezing, and the drapes were closed."

"You knew Mr. Williams for a long time?"

Greg got a faraway look in his eyes. "Yes. We served in the same unit for years. He was my best friend. I'll miss him." He slumped and lowered his head.

"What kind of business were you in?"

"Military. Army." The words were like a physical cue. His spine straightened the moment he said them.

Tom shook his head. "No, I mean now. Currently."

"Sometimes we bought and sold bikes or ran tours." Greg shrugged.

"Do you know anything about the meeting he had scheduled this morning?"

"No. He didn't mention it to me." His brow furrowed.

"Can you tell me your whereabouts today?"

"I played golf this morning, then met my wife in the bar. We played some slot machines after lunch, then returned to the room just before the maid started screaming."

"I'll need times and witnesses if you have them."

"Yes, of course. I'll write them down for you." He got up and retrieved a pen and notebook from a drawer in the dining area. Then sat back down and began to make a list.

"Do you have any idea why someone might want to murder Mr. Williams?"

Greg seemed to deflate before his eyes.

"None at all. He was a great guy. I don't know what we'll do without him." He cleared his throat.

"Thank you, sir. I'm sorry for your loss." They shook hands. "Is your wife available to speak with me now?"

"Yes, I'll call her."

Greg went into the bedroom, and Lizzie came out. She was not what Tom expected. She wore an expensive black dress and fine jewelry. Her hair was done up in a sleek French twist, and her makeup had probably been impeccable before she started crying. She glided across the room and held out a limp hand as if she expected him to kiss it.

Tom shook her hand gently and introduced himself. "Your husband told you about what happened next door?"

"Yes. Poor Roy. Poor *Cathy*. I just can't believe it!"

"Can you think of any reason someone would want him dead?"

She jerked backward. "No! He was always so nice."

"Can you walk me through your day?"

"I left our room a little before ten and went to the bar to meet Greg."

"Did you see anyone else?"

"Yes, I almost collided with Cathy in the hallway." She fluttered her hands around.

"Did you hear any of their argument?"

Lizzie blushed a little and nodded. "Mostly, I heard Cathy. Roy was soft-spoken most of the time."

Tom was surprised when Harvey asked, "What were they arguing about?" Then he looked at Tom to make sure it was okay. Tom gave a slight nod.

"I'm not sure. I thought some of it was about a woman, but when I ran into her in the hall, she said it was about a meeting. He was trying to make her leave before she was ready."

Harvey paused his writing and leaned forward. "Maybe she was just saying that because she was embarrassed. Can you recall anything specific that you heard?"

Lizzie looked anywhere but at him. "I'm not sure."

"That's okay."

Tom waited a few seconds to see if Harvey would continue, then said, "What time did Greg meet you?"

"It was close to eleven. I had finished my Bloody Mary. He told me about his golf game, and we talked about where to have lunch."

"What did you decide on?"

"We ended up staying in the bar. They have a decent menu."

"Will the bartender remember you?"

"I imagine so. Marcus was there too."

"What time did he show up?"

"I don't know." She blushed a little. "I noticed him because the girl he was sitting with had a really annoying laugh."

Tom nodded. "What happened when you got back to your room?"

"Greg turned on the TV, and I was going to have a little nap, but then the screaming started. I was scared, so Greg said he'd see what was going on."

"Did you leave the room?"

She shook her head. "No, he said to stay here and lock the door."

"Did Roy and Cathy have a good marriage?"

Lizzie's eyes widened a bit. "I... I think so. They always seemed happy."

"You said you thought some of the argument was about a woman. Can you tell me what gave you that impression?"

"I just heard a name, and I thought I heard the word *divorce*. Cathy loved Roy, and she's grieving, so I don't want to cause her extra trouble. I might have heard wrong."

Tom rubbed his chin. "Well, thank you very much for your assistance. We won't leap to any conclusions." He handed her a card. "Please let me know if you think of anything else." He and Harvey stood, and she showed them to the door.

Tom stopped by Sam's room briefly before heading back to the station. When she answered the door, she was freshly showered and dressed in low-rise jeans and a tank top. "Sorry to bother you again."

"It's no bother." She smiled. "Would you like to come in?"

Yes, yes, yes! Tom's pulse quickened. *Stop it, you idiot.* "No, thank you. I just wondered if all of you were still planning on having dinner together this evening."

"Yes. Margaritaville at six."

"Perhaps you can tell me about it tomorrow?"

"Sure. Or later tonight? I haven't seen the strip all lit up, but I'm a little nervous walking around by myself at night." She kicked her toes against the floor and looked away.

Tom raised an eyebrow. "I would have thought you'd have a gun, as a rancher and all."

"Oh, I do. I don't want to carry it in such a crowded place, though. Someone could get hurt."

What an interesting woman. So beautiful and smart. Tom stared at her, trying to figure out what to say. "Good thinking. What kind of gun?"

"It's just a micro .28 I put in my boot when I'm out by myself at the ranch. It saved my life a few months ago." She went to her safe and opened it, then walked back to the door and handed it to him.

"This might be the tiniest gun I've ever seen."

"Girl sized." Sam laughed. "I don't want to kill anyone; just slow them down so I can get away." She took the gun back and stuck it in her back pocket.

"Shall we meet outside at nine?"

"That sounds great! Thank you!"

Tom met Harvey in the lobby, and they walked to their unmarked car without speaking. After they got in and buckled up, Tom asked, "Thoughts?"

"It still could be Mrs. Williams… It's probably someone in their group, right?"

"Almost certainly, but it's a big group. We'll know more after we've spoken with all of them."

They were quiet for the rest of the trip. Tom appreciated Harvey letting him have time to think before their meeting.

Chapter 6

Tom pulled into an open parking space in front of the station, then he and Harvey made their way inside. The station lobby, always busy, was filled with every type of person imaginable, standing around, filling out forms, and sleeping on benches. The cacophony of dozens of phones and voices added to the controlled chaos. Mostly ignored, Tom and Harvey made their way to a meeting room where the crime scene analysts, responding officers, medical pathologist, and captain were all seated around a long, narrow table. Remnants of donuts and coffee sat in the middle. A lone computer sat on a second, smaller table located beneath a large television screen.

"Nice of you to join us." the captain said with a wink. "Have a donut." He chuckled at Harvey's downcast expression. "What do we have so far?"

Mike picked up his preliminary pathology report and pushed his glasses up as Tom and Harvey took their seats. "Time of death is hard to determine because of the unusually cold room. I will know better when I open him up."

Harvey picked up the small piece of donut left in the box. "His wife left at ten, and the body was found at one, which narrows it down."

"Unless she killed him," said Tom, flipping open his notepad.

Claire looked at her notes. "There was also a smashed watch on his arm that read 11:30."

"Which is odd." Tom rubbed his chin.

"Why is that odd?" Captain Rice asked.

"There were no other signs of a struggle." Tom shrugged.

"And why turn the A/C up full blast?"

"Cause of death?"

"That, at least, is clear," Mike said, looking toward the captain. "One of the two bullet wounds to the chest."

"Murder weapon?"

"We haven't found it yet, sir, but the bullets are 9mm," Claire said.

"How are the interviews progressing?"

Tom held up ten fingers. "Ten people were traveling together. One is dead. Four others have been interviewed. One suspect tentatively eliminated." He ticked off fingers, ending with five. "Harvey and I will complete the rest tomorrow."

"Why is one eliminated?"

Tom ticked the reasons off with his fingers. "She joined the party yesterday, had never met the victim until last night, was with the widow from ten to one, and has references from law enforcement in New Mexico."

Captain Rice nodded. "Good work, everyone. Let's meet up tomorrow evening to compare notes again."

They all gathered up their things and left the room, except Tom and Captain Rice, Stewart to his friends.

He approached Tom as everyone else was leaving. "Want to grab a bite to eat, Tom?"

"Sure. Do you have somewhere in mind? Or would you like to go to Margaritaville and cast an eye on our suspects?"

"Now that sounds like fun." Stewart gave a mischievous grin. "How is Harvey's training coming along?"

"He hasn't participated in many interviews yet; mostly takes notes. But he makes suggestions and comes up with theories in between. I need to encourage him to take a more active role."

"I appreciate your willingness to work with him. I think he has a lot of potential."

Tom nodded. "I do too. I'll try harder to share." He grinned.

40

"Let's change and meet at the Flamingo in about forty minutes. I'll be less recognizable in casual clothes."

Tom and Stewart, both dressed in jeans and t-shirts, met up outside the Flamingo. "Let's go around to the patio entrance," Tom said. "I have no idea where they'll be sitting."

"Sounds good. I haven't seen any of them, so you pick our spot."

Tom spotted *Torque* right away and asked the hostess for a table in the corner where he and Stewart could see the group but weren't obvious. She handed them each a menu and bustled back to the entrance.

"So, where are they?" Stewart asked, looking around.

"Seven o'clock," Tom said, perusing the menu. "That's the grieving widow," he added, as Cathy arrived. She was weaving a little, her eyes were red and puffy, and her hair was flattened on one side. Tom noticed that everyone stopped talking and looked down at the table when she arrived, all except Sam. She stood and helped Cathy to an empty seat.

"Who's that helping her?" Stewart asked.

"That's Samantha Olivares."

"Ah. Harvey told me about her."

"What did he say?"

"Nothing." Stewart's eyes shone mischievously, and Tom scowled.

"I'm not throwing him under the bus," Stewart chuckled.

"I think you already have."

The waitress approached the table and took their orders. Tom ordered the Southwest Chicken Salad, and Stewart opted for the Crispy Coconut Shrimp. As soon as the waitress left, Stewart asked who Tom had interviewed.

"Just the widow, Ms. Olivares, and the Scotts; that couple on Samantha's right."

"You don't know who the others are?"

41

"I have a list, so I can guess, but I haven't met them yet." Just then, Sam looked up and met Tom's eyes across the restaurant. Her mouth turned up in a brief smile before she looked down at her plate. Tom lost his train of thought.

Stewart watched the interaction and smiled. "She's very beautiful."

"What?"

"Samantha. I can see the attraction."

"No, it's nothing."

"Is she a suspect?"

"No, but she's connected to the case."

"Tom."

Tom looked at him.

"You haven't shown interest in anyone or anything outside of work since... for years. It's okay to have feelings."

"Thank you, sensei," Tom mumbled.

When the waitress returned with their food, they thanked her and turned their attention back to the table of suspects. Just before they were served, Cathy rose and stumbled toward the door. Lizzie Scott hurried after her, then returned to the table momentarily before following Cathy. Everyone started talking and whispering.

"I wish I was a fly on the wall," Tom gestured with his fork.

"I wish you were too." Stewart laughed. "I'm not taking any chances with a fly swatter."

The restaurant was colorful and noisy. Sam tried hard to concentrate on her meal and the conversation around her, but a fake volcano erupted, along with booming music and applause from the other diners. She looked up to see Cathy standing, swaying slightly.

"I need to leave."

Lizzie took her elbow. "Would you like to get your dinner to go?"

Cathy shook off her hand and waved her off, stumbling toward the door.

Sam stood too. "Should I go with her?"

Lizzie's eyes darted from Sam to Cathy. Her hands fluttered. "No, I'll go. See if you can get them to wrap up both of our dinners, okay?"

Sam nodded and watched her catch up with Cathy and help her out of the restaurant. She glanced quickly at Tom to see if he noticed. He nodded imperceptibly.

The others—except for Greg and Marcus—immediately let loose with their conjectures. Greg scowled and pressed his lips together.

Marcus studied everyone's face. "One of them did it," he whispered in Sam's ear. "Don't be alone with any of them until the police figure out who."

"But why would any of them want him dead?" she whispered back.

He shrugged and shook his head.

"What are you two lovebirds whispering about?" Dani asked. "Do you know something the rest of us don't?"

"Lovebirds." Rachel snorted. "That's a good one."

Everyone looked at her.

"What? He doesn't like women."

Marcus gaped at her.

"If that's what you think, then why do you follow him around like a lovesick puppy?" Dani asked.

"I've been testing him, and I was going to tell Roy." She flung her napkin on the table. "I bet he killed Roy because Roy found out."

"Why would he care?" Sam asked.

Rachel shrugged.

"That's a lot of ugly coming out of your mouth," Greg said finally. "Why don't you just leave?"

Dani opened her mouth to chime in, but Pedro put his hand on her arm.

Cal, who had been unusually silent, said, "Someone is a thief. Find the thief, and you'll find the murderer." He stabbed his potato.

Everyone stared at him before all speaking at once.

"Thief?" Rachel said.

"How do you know something was stolen?" Marcus asked.

Pedro picked up a roll. "What did they steal?"

Cal shrugged. "Roy was making money somehow."

They all went quiet. *Could that be true? Was Roy murdered for money? Who did it then? Was it one of my friends?* They looked around at each other and began to wonder if one of them was not who they seemed.

"Is this the end of *Torque*?" Rachel asked. "Roy was the glue that held us together. He was always the peacekeeper. Will we all split up now?"

Her question was met with silence. No one had an answer to that. Sam felt she was too new to comment.

When the waiter returned with their meals, Sam took hers and said, "Could you please put these two in 'to-go' boxes?"

"Mine too, please," Greg said. "I'll deliver the other two on my way to the room.".

"If you'll excuse me," Sam said, rising from her seat, "I need to use the restroom." She made her way through the crowded restaurant and spun around when she felt a hand on her shoulder. When she saw it was Tom, her muscles relaxed, and she smiled.

"Do you want to change our meeting time to eight?" he asked in a voice low enough that only she could hear.

"Yes, please. It's miserable over there."

"See you then." He disappeared into the men's room.

"Who was that?" Rachel asked from behind her.

Sam shrugged and went into the ladies' room. Rachel followed close behind and kept asking her questions until she got irritated.

"Rachel, last night you felt what it was like to be humiliated during a group dinner. Why would you turn around and do it to someone else tonight? If you have a problem with Marcus, couldn't you speak to him privately?"

Rachel narrowed her eyes at Sam. "It's not the same. I don't expect you to understand, Miss Perfect. Maybe you were in it with him."

Dani entered the restroom. "In what?"

Sam sighed. "I'm going back to the table."

On her way back, Sam saw Cal and Marcus standing near the bar in deep conversation. She couldn't hear what they were saying, but Cal looked angry. He poked a finger at Marcus' chest, and the bartender walked over to intervene.

Back at the table, Sam's dinner and drink had been cleared. She could almost feel the steam coming out of her ears. She went over to the waiters' station, where the waitstaff were gossiping. After tapping her toe and being ignored for a few seconds, Sam leveled her frustration at her waiter. "Excuse me."

Several pairs of eyes turned in her direction.

"I went to the restroom, and my food and drink disappeared. I would like them back."

"I'm sorry, ma'am. I thought you had left. Can I bring you a new one?"

"Yes. Thank you. Do you know what it was?"

The waiter looked down. "Yes, ma'am."

Sam walked back to the table and sat down.

Pedro smirked at her. "Missing something?" She just stared at him until he looked away.

The waiter came to the table with a fresh drink and apologized. "I'll bring a new plate as soon as it's ready. It's on the house."

"Thank you," she said with a smile. When she looked at Pedro, her smile disappeared. *I wonder if Marcus is right. Am I in danger? Why would Pedro target me?*

45

Everyone else had left by the time Sam got her food so Tom, having said goodnight to Stewart, joined her at her table. "What happened over here?"

Sam shook her head. "I don't even know where to begin." She lifted her fork and paused. "There are overt words and actions, and covert thoughts and action." She took a bite and chewed for a minute while she thought."

Tom waited patiently for her to process.

"Rachel and Dani make their little digs. Constantly."

"What kind of things do they say?"

"They say or insinuate I'm not part of the group, that I don't know them. They dig at each other and at Marcus about his sexuality, and since we're friends, I get some of that too." Sam took another bite. "Would you like to try this? It's quite good."

"What is it?"

"Fish and Chips."

"It looks pretty good, but I just ate."

Sam nodded as she chewed. "Anyway, at the table tonight, Marcus told me to be careful because someone at the table killed Roy. Then Cal said something about... how did he say it? Something has been stolen, and if we find the thief, we'll find the murderer. When everyone asked what had been stolen, he said Roy had been making money doing something."

"Sounds like a pretty lively discussion."

"Yeah. Then when I went to the restroom, Pedro told the waiter to go ahead and clear my place, so I came back to find my dinner gone."

Tom just sat quietly and listened.

"They are not nearly as friendly as I thought. I won't be continuing with them after this."

"I'm sorry you aren't enjoying your trip."

"It's not all bad." She grinned. "I did join a rather unfriendly bunch and get involved in a murder investigation, but I've also met some interesting people and got a chance to visit Las Vegas."

"Do you like Vegas so far?"

"I'm not really sure. I'm not a gambler, and it's very busy. Maybe you can show me the upside." She put her napkin on the table. "Are you ready to show me the neon lights?"

"Absolutely." He stood and smiled, indicating the door. "Right this way."

They stopped by the cashier's desk to see if Sam owed anything and then walked out onto the strip.

Chapter 7

Sam's first view of the Flamingo at night left her momentarily speechless, and then she laughed. "I thought it was pink during the day!"

"Do you like pink?" Tom asked.

"Not particularly," Sam laughed, "but the Flamingo certainly has plenty of it. Where are we headed?"

"I thought we could walk down to the Bellagio first. They have fountains and botanical gardens."

Sam walked along next to him, feeling his energy like an electrical current. She wondered if he could feel it too. She looked at him out of the corner of her eye now and then. He was confident in an unassuming way, about her height but much more muscular. His wavy brown hair had a tendency to fall across his forehead, and his bright, blue eyes were expressive like sunshine and shadows.

Tom looked at her like she was the only other person on the planet. The crowds around them melted and disappeared until she and Tom were alone in their own little bubble.

When they got to the Fountains of Bellagio, her attention was diverted by the sheer beauty of them. The water, lights, and music created intricate, ever-changing patterns. She and Tom sat and watched for half an hour before going inside to wander around the botanical gardens.

"Which was your favorite?" Tom asked.

"The fountains. I've never seen anything like them before. How about you?"

"I've seen them many times before but watching them with you was like seeing them for the first time. I love seeing the marvel and enjoyment in your eyes."

The Cardinal, The Fat Boy & The Flamingo

Sam looked into his eyes and saw the sun shining there. Something stirred deep inside her, a powerful emotion she hadn't felt before.

When they left the gardens, Tom said, "We have several options. We can take a bus tour, look around Fremont street, go to a dance club or bowling, zip line, ride the *High Roller*. What interests you?"

"Let's look around Fremont Street," she said. "Then we can do whatever you want."

"Fremont Street it is," he said, taking her hand in his. His hand was large and warm. She could feel a tingle from her fingertips to her toes. She held on tight for fear of losing that feeling.

They walked around, checking out the light shows and music venues until it started getting late.

"Can I take you on the *High Roller* before we head back?" Tom asked.

"That sounds perfect."

They didn't speak much on the way back to the Linq Promenade. Sam felt a little like she was floating. Tom's presence and the touch of his hand were at once exciting and reassuring. She looked around at the bright neon lights and crowd of mostly-smiling faces. The smells of food, cigarettes, sweat, and alcohol assailed her nose, and the ever-present sound of music put a spring in her step. She looked at Tom and caught him watching her with a soft smile on his face. She smiled back as they joined the line for the High Roller.

They boarded the enclosed cabin, and the higher they went, the tighter she held onto his hand until pausing 500 feet in the air, she felt like she was at the top of the world. "I came up here during the day," she said, "but this is completely different. It's magical."

He looked at her and said, "It is."

She thought he might kiss her, suspect or not, but he didn't. He kissed the back of her hand when they got back to the Flamingo,

49

and he wished her goodnight, not entering the lobby. She turned back as she entered, and he was still standing there, watching her go.

Tom walked back to his personal vehicle. He hadn't told Sam that he was a Harley aficionado, but he was impressed with her Fat Boy. He rode a sleek, black Softail Heritage Classic. As he drove home, he allowed himself to daydream a little, and he smiled at the thought of a road trip with Sam.

Pulling into the garage beneath his apartment, Tom rode the elevator to the fourth floor and let himself inside his apartment. He didn't have plants or pets because his hours were erratic at best.

He flung himself on his bed, fully clothed, and expected to sleep soundly for six hours. Sleep eluded him that night. Images of Sam's sparkling eyes and the feel of her hand in his kept replaying in his mind. He had never met a woman like her before; he didn't even know such a woman existed.

Tom got up at dawn. He hadn't slept but somehow felt energized and ready to tackle the day. He showered, put on a fresh suit, and walked to the station, as he did every morning when he was working a case.

Harvey strolled in half an hour later bearing coffee. He juggled the coffee, setting Tom's on his desk and managing to set his own down with minimal spillage.

"Ready to get cracking?" Tom asked.

Harvey tilted his head to the side and looked at Tom. "Is there something different about you this morning?"

"Nope." Tom smiled.

"There is. What happened last night?"

"I might have walked around the strip with a beautiful, blue-haired woman."

"A beautiful suspect, you mean?"

Tom's eyes stormed. "She's been cleared. I checked her references."

"Still. You always tell me not to trust anyone."

Tom frowned a little at that. "You have a point, but I do like her." His shoulders slumped a little.

"Don't be like that. I'm sure everything will work out. What's our plan for the day?"

"We still have five people to interview. I have made appointments with each of them. And the autopsy should be done by this afternoon."

"Do you think his wife killed him?"

Tom tilted his head slightly and thought. "That would be most obvious. As you pointed out, she might have had a motive, depending on what they fought about. She had opportunity since they shared a room. And she had means; his own gun."

"But what about her alibi?" He took a sip of coffee. "Out shopping with your blue-haired beauty."

"We still don't know the time of death, but the security footage shows he had multiple visitors after she left. The watch seems too convenient, and the air conditioning..."

"About the A/C." Harvey compressed his lips. "Mike can tell the time of death based on how close the victim's body temperature is to the temperature of the room, right?"

"Possibly." Tom looked at him questioningly.

"So wouldn't turning up the air make it look like the victim was killed earlier?"

Tom shrugged. "There are other ways to find out."

"But..." Harvey spread out his hands, "If it was the wife, wouldn't she want it to look like later when she had an alibi?"

Tom shook his head. "Good questions, Harve. The problem with that kind of conjecture is that we don't know what the murderer was thinking or what he or she knows about discovering time of death. It will be better if we interview everyone first and follow the clues."

Harvey nodded. "So, who's first?"

"We have a breakfast interview with Cal Lenox at eight. Are you ready to go?"

Tom and Harvey waited for Cal at a table in a relatively quiet corner at the Circus Circus buffet. They had already filled their plates and begun eating so they could pause and ask questions. They watched Cal as he moved through the line, unabashedly flirting with every female whether they appeared interested or not. He also spoke with the kitchen staff as he went.

Cal joined them at the table, set his plate down, and shook Tom's hand.

"This is Detective Harvey Brother," Tom said.

Cal looked around. "This is not very private."

Tom nodded. "True. But you chose the location, and it's not very crowded yet."

He focused his attention on Tom. "You were out with Sam last night."

Tom looked at Cal's interesting food choices. Nothing with dairy. *This guy is pretty slick. He's trying to divert attention away from himself.*

"Also true." *I wonder if he's interested in Sam.* "Are you ready to begin?"

"That's not very professional, is it? Dating a suspect." Cal looked Tom in the eye with a hard expression.

Tom sighed. "She is not a suspect."

"Why not?" His face took on a shade of purple, and he gripped his fork fiercely. She arrives, and the next day our leader is killed?"

Tom was rapidly losing his patience. "Mr. Lenox," he said sternly, "you can either allow us to interview you, or I can take you to the station and have someone else interview you. Your choice."

Harvey looked startled but said nothing.

"Fine. Fine." Cal put his hands up. "Go ahead."

"Did you get along well with the victim?"

Cal took a big bite of sausage. When he finished chewing, he said, "Yes, of course. He was a great guy."

"Do you have any idea who might have wanted him dead or why?"

Cal mumbled around his food. "I don't know. Jealousy maybe? Theft?"

"Could you be a little more specific?"

"He might have had an affair with Rachel, so Marcus might have been jealous. Roy was the leader. Maybe someone wanted his spot. He was making money from something. Maybe someone wanted that something. I don't know anything specific."

Tom paused and raised his eyebrows at Harvey, who was taking notes. He knew their non-verbal communication would worry Cal.

"Where were you yesterday between ten and one?"

"In the casino at the Flamingo. I'm sure the cocktail waitresses will remember me."

"You didn't see any of the others?"

"No." He grabbed the saltshaker.

"Do you have a gun?"

Cal shook his head as he chewed.

"Where do you consider home?"

"I don't have one, currently. I might stay in Vegas if *Torque* splits up."

Harvey stopped writing. "Do you think they will?"

"I have no idea, but it's a possibility."

"What do you do for a living?" Tom asked.

Cal shrugged. "This and that."

"Such as?"

"Sometimes I do some work for Pedro. I'm a licensed broker and an investor. Sometimes I work as a consultant."

"How long have you been riding with *Torque?*"

Cal thought about that, repositioning his napkin. "About six months. I've been friends with Pedro for a long time."

Tom stood. "Thank you for your cooperation. Please, let me know if you think of anything else."

"Sure." Cal looked a little surprised but covered it by returning his attention to his breakfast.

Harvey stood as well and followed Tom through the buffet to

the casino exit. "What an unpleasant guy," he said as they walked away.

"He's pretty slick. I'm guessing he has quite a few secrets he's not sharing."

"Do you think he could be the murderer?"

"Not really. I could be wrong, but I'm guessing he's a different kind of low life."

Harvey thought about that. "Like a blackmailer?"

Tom nodded but rubbed his chin. "We'll need to have each of their rooms searched."

"The weapon?"

"Yes. It seems several are missing. And perhaps we will find something worth stealing."

Harvey placed the call to request search warrants as they walked back to the Flamingo for their second interview.

Marcus Rhodes was sitting at the bar, talking to the bartender when they arrived. Tom approached and introduced himself. The bartender winked at Marcus and moved farther down the bar.

"Let's join my colleague at that table over there," Tom suggested.

Marcus shrugged and followed him.

Once they were seated, Tom said, "Roy Williams was your uncle. Did he invite you to join Torque?"

Marcus swirled his drink. "Yes. He said he wanted me to get involved in the family business."

"And what was that?"

"I don't know." Marcus shifted in his chair. "He didn't tell me."

"Did anyone else know he was your uncle?"

"I don't think so."

Tom lifted an eyebrow. "Not even his wife?"

Marcus shook his head. "I think they were having problems."

"Marital problems?"

"Yeah." He furrowed his brow.

54

"What makes you say that?"

Marcus shook his head. "Cathy was jealous of Rachel, and Roy started being more secretive. It was just a feeling. Greg might be able to tell you more."

"Why is that?"

"They were lifelong friends. Greg knew him better than anyone," Marcus had a twinge of disdain in his voice that made Tom sit up and take notice.

"How long have you been with *Torque?*"

Marcus swirled his drink again. "About four months."

"Is there anyone who disliked Roy?"

"I don't know. I didn't hear anyone say so."

Tom looked at Marcus sharply. "Where were you yesterday between ten and one."

"I was here."

"Did you see Greg and Lizzie?"

"Yes." Marcus suddenly spoke with authority. "She left for about half an hour, and after she left, he left too. He asked the bartender to watch their drinks."

Tom leaned forward. "How do you know that?"

Marcus shifted in his chair. "He and I are... friends. When they came back, I made sure they saw me sitting with a sexy young woman. Roy wouldn't have liked my *preferences.*"

Tom looked at Harvey. "Did anyone else know?"

"It's not a big secret, but Rachel outed me last night at dinner."

Tom folded his napkin into small squares. "We haven't spoken with her yet."

"Yeah. Have fun." Marcus grimaced.

Tom knocked on Rachel's door and was glad Harvey was with him when she answered. Wearing a bikini, she clearly thought she would be seducing someone. Harvey gulped audibly, and Rachel smiled. "Hello, Ms. Simon. I'm Detective Thomas Cork, and this is Detective Harvey Brother. May we come in?"

"Of course, I've been expecting you." She strutted over to a small table by the windows. Harvey shut the door behind them and followed Tom into the room. "Have a seat. Can I get you something to drink?"

"No," Tom said. "Thank you." He sat at the table, and Harvey perched on the edge of the bed with his notebook.

"What would you like to know?"

"How long have you been with *Torque*?"

"A few months." She ran her hand through her thin blonde hair. "I met Cathy when they passed through the town where I was living."

"What town is that?"

"Austin, Texas."

"Did you know Roy well?"

"No, not really, but I liked him." Her eyes went soft, and a small smile played around her thin lips.

"Was your interest in him of a romantic nature?"

She jerked back and looked at Tom with disgust. "Ew, no! He was old enough to be my father!"

"I'm sorry if that offended you," Tom shrugged. "Can you think of any reason someone might want him dead?"

"He might have found something out about someone."

"Like what?"

She looked away. "I think Pedro is doing something illegal, and Marcus said something about theft."

"Did you follow Marcus here?"

Rachel narrowed her eyes at Tom. "Did Sam tell you that?"

"No, but I'll ask her if you think she knows something."

"I wanted to tell Roy about him." She flipped her hair. "I never got the chance."

"Why not?" Tom asked coldly. "It seems like an easy enough secret to divulge."

"I didn't think he'd believe me. Women are always all over Marcus." Rachel scowled.

"I was trying to get close enough that he'd trust me."

"It was pretty important to you."

"Yes." Her face had turned pink, and she squirmed in her chair, causing Harvey's eyes to widen slightly.

"What do you do for a living?"

"I don't work. I ended up with a large divorce settlement," Rachel said smugly.

"And where were you between ten and one yesterday?"

"I was shopping."

"Alone?" Tom asked with surprise.

"Yes."

"Is there a shopkeeper who might remember you? Any receipts?"

"I don't know." She squared her shoulders. "What's the big deal? I was just wandering around."

"Well, thank you, Ms. Simon. Give me a call if you think of anything else." He stood and handed her a card.

"I'd rather have *your* card."

Harvey blushed as he stood, and Tom held out his hand. Thank you for your assistance."

She walked them to the door and watched as they walked to the elevators.

The elevator dinged, and the doors opened. "Please don't ever make me interview her alone." Harvey shivered and shook his head as he entered and watched the doors close.

Tom chuckled. "Would you like to come with me to meet up with Sam?"

"If you don't mind."

"I don't mind; it's work-related."

Chapter 8

Sam woke at eight, had some breakfast, and went for a swim. Swimming in the morning helped her clear her head and get ready for the day. At home, riding Ghost in the morning had the same effect. It was her equivalent to meditating, alone outdoors, quiet and contemplative. As she let her muscle memory propel her, she thought of Cathy the night before. She wondered how she was doing and if Lizzie was still with her.

Once she changed out of her suit, she stopped by Cathy's room to check on her. She knocked on the door, but there was no answer. She knocked again and waited. *I hope she's okay. I should have come by sooner.* She tried one more time and then strolled back to the elevator. Dani was waiting too. "Have you seen Cathy this morning?"

"I saw her at breakfast. Why do you care?"

Sam raised her eyebrows. "Because she's my friend. I'm worried about her."

Dani stiffened. "You don't even know her. You're just being nosy."

"You're just mean to everyone, aren't you?" Sam didn't understand Dani's hostility. She seemed so friendly when they first met, but she had changed.

Dani crossed her arms. "I say it like I see it. You should just go home."

"Maybe we'll all go home, but not until the police finish their investigation."

"Cathy doesn't have a home. Roy sold it." Sam thought she caught a glimmer of sadness in Dani's demeanor, but it was gone before she could analyze it, replaced by that hard, coldness she had recently been subjected to.

The elevator stopped, and Dani got off on her floor. Sam thought about what she'd said about Roy selling their home. When she stepped off the elevator in the lobby, she almost collided with Tom.

"Whoa." He put his hands on her shoulders to stop her. "You look miles away."

"Sorry!" Sam snapped to attention. "I'm glad it's you I almost trampled and not some little old lady." She smiled. "Hello, Detective Brother."

"Hello, Ms. Olivares. You can call me Harvey."

"Only if you call me Sam." She smiled at him. He seemed so shy and polite; she wanted to hug him.

"Where are we headed?" Tom asked.

"I saw a coffee bar down that way." Sam pointed in the direction of *Cup of Cappuccino*. "I think they have patio seating."

"Sounds good."

They found a relatively quiet table at the edge of the patio. The glassed-in room looked like an outdoor patio, with plenty of leafy green plants and sunlight, but it was climate controlled and less noisy than an open patio. Once they got settled and each had a sip of their coffee, Tom asked, "What did you find out at dinner last night?"

"Well, I've already told you most of it. Cathy was drunk, Marcus told me to be careful, Dani called us lovebirds, Rachel told the whole table Marcus is gay and said he probably killed Roy because he found out, Cal announced that someone was a thief, and Pedro told the waiter to clear my plate when I went to the ladies' room. They were all horrible."

"So, nothing concrete, just sniping at each other?" Tom asked.

"Pretty much. Today, I stopped by Cathy's room, but there was no answer. I saw Dani on the way down and asked her about Cathy. Dani told me Cathy was at breakfast. Then she said I was just nosy and should go home."

Harvey wrinkled his nose. "That doesn't sound very nice."

"She is particularly mean to Rachel, so it's not just me."

"Well, we are almost done with our first round of interviews. We just have Pedro and Dani left, but I'm not sure we're any closer to solving the crime. Is there anyone you don't think could have done it?"

"I don't think Cathy could have done it since we were together the whole time. I suppose anyone else could have gone to their room after we left. I really have no idea. Does anyone have an alibi?"

"Yes and no. We still have some checking to do."

Taking his cue from Tom, Harvey asked, "I know this is very subjective, but you've spent a little time with all of them. Is there anyone you *could* picture as the murderer?"

Sam raised her eyebrows at that. She paused a moment in thought. "Greg is a military man. His gun went missing, and he was staying next door. But they were also great friends. Cal is creepy, but I think that's just a misguided attempt at being a ladies' man. Pedro seems kind of sinister, but I don't know him at all. Something's up with Rachel. Maybe she loved him. Maybe she hated him. I could see her pulling the trigger in anger. Cathy, if I'm honest, is a very emotional person. If we hadn't been together and I hadn't seen her so gutted by his death, I would say she might be capable of doing it."

Tom was impressed by her observations. "What about the other three?"

"I could be wrong because anyone who feels really threatened might be capable of murder, but I feel like the other three are much too self-absorbed to bother, especially Lizzie and Dani."

"Marcus?" Tom leaned forward.

"Did you find out who his uncle is?"

"Roy was his uncle," Harvey said.

"Then, I don't think it was him. He would benefit more from keeping him alive."

"Thanks, Sam. Harvey's right. Even though it's not very scientific, personal observation can add another dimension to the puzzle." Tom was astonished at Sam's insight. *I wonder if Sergeant Mickelson and her cousin, Jack, knew how lucky they were to have her on their team.*

"I don't know everything you've found out, so I'm just taking them at face value." Sam smiled, and her eyes twinkled, and Tom felt like she was projecting her special energy to him alone. He had an urge to put his arms around her and tell her how special she was, but he ended up saying, "We'd better get to our next interviews. It was good seeing you."

They all rose and shook hands. Tom looked back as they walked away and saw her watching them. He gave her a little wave and a wink, then turned his attention back to Harvey.

When they got to the elevator, Harvey turned to Tom. "She's pretty great."

"She keeps surprising me." Tom pictured Sam pondering a puzzle and the look she got when she solved it. "That was smart, reversing the question. She came up with quite a few good observations."

Harvey's brow furrowed. "They don't really help narrow things down, though."

"They might at some point. It's important to look at a problem from more than one angle."

They exited the elevator on the 19th floor and knocked on Pedro and Dani's door. Pedro answered, so Tom introduced himself and Harvey. They shook hands and entered a suite much like the crime scene, but not nearly as neat.

"Dani's in the bedroom. I thought you might like to talk to us separately."

"Yes. Thank you," Tom said.

"Have a seat."

They all sat in the living room area, and Tom leaned forward as if confiding in Pedro. "Could you tell me how well you knew Roy?"

"Fairly well. I was friends with Greg first, but we've been riding together for about a year and a half."

"Can you think of a reason why anyone would want him dead?"

"No. I've been thinking about that." Pedro scratched his whiskers. "Maybe it was a mistake? A stranger? We *all* liked him. Unless it was that crazy woman, Rachel. But I think she might have had an affair with him, so even that doesn't make sense."

Tom nodded. "What if his wife found out about an affair?"

Pedro pressed his lips into a thin line. "She would have been plenty mad, but she would've kicked Rachel out of *Torque*, not killed her old man."

"What do you do for a living?" Tom was looking for a reaction, and Pedro was well rehearsed, but his shoulders tensed, and he looked up sharply.

"I own a motorcycle repair shop in Pasadena."

"California?"

"Yes. My son is running it while we're on the road."

"Some of your group think you might be doing something illegal."

Pedro smiled like a shark. "That's just my tough guy persona. I like to keep it that way so they don't mess with me."

Tom nodded. "Where were you between ten and one yesterday?"

"I was doing some work; Skyping with my son, making sure I have something to go home to." Pedro's eyes flicked to Harvey taking notes.

"Thank you for your cooperation. Perhaps you can share your son's number with Detective Brother, and we'll speak with Dani now."

"Yeah, no problem." He nodded, stood, and walked to the bedroom, flicking his thumb toward the detectives as he entered.

Dani stepped out, swinging her hips in stiletto heels, and reminded Tom of the biker girls in an old 50's beach movie with tight leather pants and cherry red lips. Both men stood.

"Please, sit." she purred. "Would you like something to drink?"

"No, thank you," Tom said.

Harvey shook his head and snapped his mouth shut.

She sat across from them and smiled. "How can I help you?"

Tom sat and motioned for Harvey to do the same. "Did you know Roy well?"

"Not really. I mostly spend time with Pedro or the other women."

"Where were you between ten and one yesterday?"

"I'd rather not say." She crossed her arms.

"You don't want to provide an alibi?"

She leaned forward and whispered, "I don't want Pedro to know where I was."

"Maybe it can be our little secret," Tom whispered back.

Dani looked at the bedroom door. "I went to see a doctor about a nose job."

"Could I have the name and address?" He carefully suppressed any sign of surprise or mirth. This was obviously something that was important to her.

"Yes, of course. Please don't tell Pedro. He'll think it's stupid, but I hate my nose."

"I imagine he loves you just the way you are."

Dani smiled.

"Do you know anything about his business?"

"Like what?" She studied her long, pink nails.

"Like what he does for a living?"

She flipped her hair. "Some kind of repair shop."

"Is he involved in anything illegal?"

She sat up straighter and quickly glanced at Harvey, writing in his notebook. "Of course not!"

"Can you think of any reason someone might want to kill Roy?"

"No... well, he might have been having an affair." Her eyes squinted. "If I ever found out Pedro had someone on the side, he would be very sorry."

"Got it." Tom raised an eyebrow.

"I hope he is smart enough not to go down that road."

She stiffened and scowled. "He'd better not."

Tom watched her face relax back into a smile as she turned her focus back to her audience. *Fascinating.*

"Thank you for your cooperation. If you could get me that doctor's name and address, we'll get out of your hair."

She fluffed said hair and moved across the room to get a business card out of her purse.

Tom stood and read the card. "How did you get there?"

"I walked."

He looked at her shoes. "That's pretty far."

"I did some shopping on the way." She flung her hands out in a gesture that Tom interpreted as no big deal.

Heading toward the door, Harvey tripped and blushed.

"Thank you again, Ms. Golden."

They got back on the elevator, and Tom laughed. "Did you get any notes at all, Harve?"

Harvey blushed again.

Chapter 9

After her meeting with Tom and Harvey, Sam went to visit the Flamingo Wildlife Habitat. The concrete path wound around the hotel grounds. She wasn't alone and initially, she was distracted by the other guests. Some bounced around and made a lot of noise, especially families with young children. Sam strolled slowly, focusing on the verdant beauty of the gardens and allowing it to pull her in. She listened to the birds chattering and waterfalls splashing into the small river. She watched the birds' antics and the water moving under the bridges she crossed. It was hot outside, but the water and the shade provided some relief. Sam stopped in a quiet alcove, letting the flowing water soothe her as she watched a pair of Chilean flamingos.

"They say flamingos represent a need to look at something from a different perspective."

Sam spun around, eyes wide and heart beating hard at the sudden interruption. When she saw it was Marcus, her muscles relaxed. Hand on her heart, she said, "Why did you do that?" Then she looked back at the flamingos. "Is that true?"

"Yeah." They stood there quietly for a few minutes.

Sam turned to him. "Did you follow me here?"

Marcus shuffled his feet and looked sheepish. "I did, but I waited a while so you could enjoy the gardens. I like to come here in the morning and meditate."

Sam's eyes widened. "You are full of surprises."

Marcus looked down at his feet. "We all have outer shells we show the world. Then there's another part of us we keep private."

Sam nodded.

"You don't seem to be putting on a front. You feel pretty authentic." He looked at her searchingly.

"I don't always share my internal struggles, but you're right. I don't pretend to be something I'm not."

"Can I confide in you?"

She crossed her arms. "If it's not about the murder." *Don't let it be about the murder. I don't want to be any more involved than I already am.*

"Not directly, but it could have something to do with it. I'm not sure. He ran a hand through his hair. "I need some advice."

Sam noticed he was missing his charming grin. His eyes lacked their mischievous sparkle. They were deep and flat like a winter lake. She looked around. "Do you want to talk here?"

"No, can we go sit in a corner in the bar?"

"We could. Or you can come up to my room."

Marcus shook his head and put his hands up.

"I'm not hitting on you." She chuckled.

"Sorry. It just happens all the time."

"The bar is fine."

They went in and sat at a table in a far corner where they wouldn't be overheard.

"Have you eaten?" Marcus asked.

"Not since breakfast."

"Hold on a second." Marcus walked up to the bar and spoke to the bartender, returning with a couple of menus. He handed one to Sam and sat back down.

A waitress came to the table after a few minutes and asked what they would like to order.

"I'd like a burger and fries. And a frozen strawberry margarita."

Marcus laughed. "I think you might have a margarita problem. I'll have the same, but with a side salad instead of fries."

Marcus leaned forward once the waitress left. "I lied to the police."

Samantha's eyes widened, and she leaned in too. "About what?"

"They knew Roy was my uncle, and I told them he had asked me here to help with the family business. That was true." He unrolled the napkin holding his silverware, then rolled it up again. "But then I told them he hadn't told me what that business was."

"Why? Is it illegal?"

"No, no!" He shook his head violently. "Roy dealt in rare and valuable coins. No one knew except me and maybe Greg, not even Cathy. The coins are missing."

Sam nodded. "And you want them back."

"Well, yes, but the safe was open when they found him. I don't know if he kept them there, but…."

Sam grabbed his hand. "The person who has them could be the murderer. You should tell the police."

"Then I'll never get them back. I have a lot of money tied up in those coins." He leaned back, and his shoulders slumped.

Sam pursed her lips and thought about that as the waitress brought their orders and asked if they wanted anything else. When she left, Marcus said, "I want to search Greg's room."

"If he has the coins, wouldn't he keep them in the safe?"

"Probably, but I can get in the safe. Will you help me?"

"What can I do?"

"Help me find out when they'll be away from the room and keep lookout. If you're in there with me, you can also be a witness that he had them and that I didn't take anything else."

"If he's the killer, that could be very dangerous. Are you sure we can't tell the police? Or at least have them nearby?"

Marcus shook his head. "Please. Will you help me? You can have them nearby for some other reason."

Sam's pulse had quickened. She wanted to help, if just to keep Marcus safe, but she knew it was dangerous. She also knew Tom would not want her to get involved.

"Please?"

They were interrupted when Dani sidled up to their table. "Well, well, well. What do we have here? I knew I was right about you two."

67

"What do you want, Dani?" Marcus frowned at her.

"Do you mind if I join you?" She sat down before they could answer and stole a fry from Sam's plate.

"Your conversation looked intense. Sam looked worried. Are you trying to blackmail her?"

Marcus frowned. "I'm not, but if I was, explain to me how that would be your business."

"Sam's my friend, of course. Aren't you?"

Sam stared at Dani incredulously. "Since last time I saw you, you told me I should go home; I'm guessing that would be a hard no."

"Aww. I thought you were everybody's friend. Now I feel bad." She smiled and took another fry.

Sam pushed the plate toward her.

"Oh no, only one or two." Dani licked her fingers and took another fry. "I don't want to get fat."

"If you're going to put your fingers in my food without asking, you can just have the whole plate." She waved down the waitress. "Could I have another side of fries, please?"

"Of course. Is there anything wrong with those?"

"No, they're fine. Thanks. You can bring a to-go container for my friend here."

The waitress nodded and left.

"What's the matter with you?" Dani screeched. "All I did was take a fry or two, and you're making a federal case of it."

Sam stared at her. The three sat in silence until the waitress came back with a plate of fries and a to-go container. Sam put the plate of fries on her opposite side and poured the ones from her first plate into the box, before handing it to Dani. "I told you. I don't want them. They're cold anyway." Sam resumed eating her lunch.

"Go away," Marcus said.

Dani got a pouty look on her face and leaned toward Marcus. "I have something I need to talk to someone about."

"Go talk to Pedro."

"It's about him."

68

Marcus looked at her. Sam kept eating.

"Well? What is it?"

"I just want to talk to you. Not her." She indicated Sam with her thumb.

"I'm having lunch with her right now," he stuck a pickle in his mouth, "and you're interrupting."

Dani hugged herself and let out a breath. "I lied to the police, and now I'm scared."

"What did you lie about?" Marcus raised his eyebrows

"I told them I didn't know anything about Pedro's business." She looked down at her fingernails.

"The chop shop?"

Dani made a round oh with her lips. "You knew?"

"He tried to give Roy a great deal on a Harley, and Greg told Roy not to buy it."

"You didn't tell the police, did you?"

Marcus shrugged and took another bite of his burger. "It's not any of my business, but it's not a big secret since Greg knows too."

"Ok. Well, I'm not going to be the one who tells them," Dani said. "It's nothing to do with the murder."

"How do you know that?" Sam finally spoke. "Maybe Roy threatened to call the police."

Dani sneered. "Like I said, you don't know us. Just butt out."

"You have a nice day, Dani." Sam wiggled her fingers in a mock wave and smiled sweetly.

Dani got up and started to stomp off, then returned for the box of fries. She snatched it off the table and stormed out of the bar.

Sam and Marcus chuckled and finished their lunches.

"You could have just told her to stop eating your fries."

"I know, but that wasn't the point. She made a big deal about us not being friends and then just took them without asking. And licked her fingers. Eww." Sam made a face.

"So, if I stole a fry, you wouldn't mind?"

"Not at all. Go ahead." She pushed her plate toward him.

"I didn't want them all, anyway. I was just making a point."

He chuckled and picked out a fry. "How are we going to figure out what time Greg and Lizzie will be out of their room tomorrow?"

Sam paused and tilted her head to one side. "Maybe we'll find out at dinner tonight, if anyone shows up."

"Last night was painful."

"It was. We should make a code phrase for tonight. In case we need to leave."

"How about *You up for some dancing?* I'm supposed to meet Darren at Omnia, anyway, and you should see it at least once."

"Yeah, ok, but that's not really a code phrase if we're actually going dancing." Sam wagged a fry at him. "When are you guys meeting up? I could ask a friend as well."

"Like who?"

"Detective Cork," Sam said sheepishly.

"Do you think he'd meet you there?"

She shrugged. "Maybe."

"It doesn't open until 10:30, but we can always look around while we wait."

"If you ask if I'm up for some dancing, everyone will invite themselves. How about, *I'm not feeling too well?*"

"Okay. If one of us says that, we can meet in the lobby." He stood, then said, "And by the way…"

Sam looked up at him.

"You'll need to wear a dress to the club."

"Great. I guess I have to go shopping." Sam stood. "I'll see you at dinner."

Chapter 10

That evening everyone met up at Bugsy and Meyer's Steakhouse. Cathy arrived first and followed the waiter through the restaurant to a door in the back.

"Why are we back here? Is something wrong?"

"No, ma'am. Mr. Scott telephoned and requested seating in our secret speakeasy."

He led Cathy to their table. She sat and thought how presumptuous Greg had become. *He acts like he's the official leader now.*

"Would you like something to drink while you wait?"

"Yes, I'll have a smoky old fashioned." She looked up and saw Greg enter with his arm around Pedro's shoulders. They were deep in conversation like Greg and Roy used to be. Behind them, Dani and Rachel were laughing and looking back toward the entrance, waiting for Lizzie. Not a care in the world. Cal walked in with his usual swagger, then Marcus and Sam came in last. *I hate them all. If Roy and I hadn't sold the house and started traveling around with these people, he would still be alive. And they don't even care that he's gone.*

She tried to keep things light. "Hello, everyone!" But when they looked at her, she saw pity and discomfort in their eyes. *I wish I could just leave.* Looking around, she saw Sam. *She seems like such a sensible girl, other than coming to Vegas. Maybe talking to her would help. Lizzie is driving me crazy.* "Sam! Why don't you sit over here, next to me."

Sam walked over and gave her a hug. "I stopped by your room this morning, but you weren't there."

"I'm afraid I'm not very good company right now, but I've been feeling cooped up in that room." *With Lizzie.*

"Maybe we could take a little walk tomorrow. Have you been to the Wildlife Habitat?"

71

"You know what I'd like to do? I'd like to revisit that morning. Walk down the Linq Promenade, ride the *High Roller*, eat In 'N Out. I hate associating all those things with...." Cathy swallowed. "Would you do that with me?"

"Of course. I really enjoyed spending that time together."

"Oh!" Cathy looked up, surprised to see the waiter. "I'll have the rib cap and a side of mac 'n cheese."

Sam looked over the menu. "I'll have the prime rib and asparagus."

They were the last two to order, and when the waiter took their menus and left, everyone stared at them.

"What?" Cathy asked.

"You've been out of it and not talking to anyone for two days, yet here you are talking to her like you're best friends," Dani said.

"Would you prefer I go back to my room?"

Dani paled. "No! We've all just missed you. We've been worried about you."

"I know, dear." Cathy gave a sad smile. "Sometimes other people's feelings combined with our own grief become a very heavy weight to bear."

"But..."

"The best thing all of you can do for me right now is stop looking at me with pity. Stop associating me with Roy's death. Let me grieve in private and try to take my mind off it when we're together. Grief is tiring, and I'm exhausted."

Greg held up his glass. "Here's to Cathy, a strong, loving woman with a heart of gold. Cheers."

Everyone held up their glasses. "To Cathy."

Cathy smiled with tears in her eyes. "Thank you, Greg. Thank you all."

Sam leaned over and said, "I'll switch places with Dani so she can talk to you. Tomorrow, we'll go on our outing."

"Thank you, dear." Cathy smiled and watched Sam walk over to Dani and put her hand on her shoulder.

Dani's shoulders tightened, and she turned with a scowl. Once Sam explained, Dani relaxed and looked like the cat who got the cream.

Sam sat between Marcus and Pedro but didn't glance at either of them. She was taken aback by the look in Rachel's eyes. Sitting directly across the table, Rachel was staring with fierce concentration. Her eyes were squinting, jaw thrust forward, mouth turned downward in a frown. *I wonder what I did this time.* Sam sighed.

Marcus, ever the devil, swung his arm around Sam's shoulders and leaned in to whisper in her ear. "Are you receiving the extrasensory daggers Rachel's sending you?"

"I'm sure you're not helping."

He chuckled. "Are we still on for tonight?"

"Yes."

The waiter began bringing their dinners and got a little confused by the seat swapping. He was very professional and congenial, however; managing to make them feel like his favorite customers.

Marcus had ordered a couple of sides, explaining quietly to Sam that a hundred-dollar meal wasn't in line with his cash flow problem. Sam promptly cut her prime rib in half and put half on his plate. "You can give me a scoop of your mac 'n cheese if you want." She winked.

Marcus smiled. "Help yourself."

The meal was quiet by *Torque* standards. The group chatted quietly amongst themselves and watched Cathy from the corners of their eyes.

At one point, Marcus said, "Does anyone have plans tomorrow? What have you been doing to keep busy? I've started getting bored."

"You need to take up shopping, like Dani," Rachel suggested.

Dani scowled. "What do you do that's so interesting?"

"I've been going to the gym and the pool if you must know. I'm taking this time to get fit."

"Yeah, you need it." Dani grinned wickedly.

73

"All of us could probably use a little more exercise."

"Speak for yourself," Cal said. "I've been taking a lot of photos. If we stay here much longer, I'll probably turn pro."

"I go golf every morning, then meet Lizzie for breakfast. You can join me tomorrow if you like."

"What time do you tee off?" Marcus asked.

"About eight. We're usually done by ten, so that's when Lizzie and I plan to meet. By the time we're done eating and playing some slots, around noon, we go back up to the room and relax for a while."

"I'll be out late tonight, but maybe I could join you some other morning?"

"What are you doing tomorrow, Sam?" Rachel asked.

"I'm not sure yet." Sam glanced at Cathy. She wasn't sure if Cathy wanted their outing to be a secret or not.

Dinner was not as terrible as Sam had expected. Time sped by, and people began finishing their meals and making comments about calling it a night. She was surprised when Marcus leaned over and whispered, "You up for some dancing?"

Sam nodded and said, "Just a second." She stood and walked over to Cathy. Bending down, she whispered, "I'm going now. I wanted to say goodnight. Is 12:30 okay?"

Cathy smiled and nodded. "Goodnight, dear. I'll see you tomorrow."

Dani had been talking to Lizzie but swung her head around to see what she missed. She was too late.

Marcus met Sam in the lobby and promptly draped his arm across her shoulders. "Don't look now, but we have company."

"Who?"

"Rachel, of course."

"Why do you goad her like this?"

"Because she outed me at the dinner table. She's spiteful and mean. Now, everyone thinks she made it up." Marcus laughed.

"Do you really care if they all know?"

"I don't care at all. It's kind of like Dani and the French fries."

Sam grinned.

"We need to get you upstairs so you can change."

"Oh, yeah. I forgot." She eyed Marcus's black trousers and silk shirt. "I didn't want to wear it to dinner because everyone would have noticed. It's totally out of character for me."

"I know." Marcus's eyes sparkled with mischief. He walked her to the elevators and told her he'd meet her in the bar.

Sam met him twenty minutes later, dressed in a short, form-fitting dress covered in silver sequins that sparkled when they caught the light. At six feet tall, Sam didn't ordinarily wear heels of any kind, but she had found a pair of low, silver heels that matched her dress. She added some subtle makeup and glitter in her hair.

Marcus gaped when Sam walked in.

"Stop! I feel self-conscious enough." She blushed.

"You look incredible! Now I feel under dressed."

"Is it too much?"

"Absolutely not! Clubbing in Vegas is all about the glamour. You'll probably be an Instagram sensation by tomorrow."

Sam grimaced.

"Don't do that. It'll ruin the effect. Ready to go?" He held out his elbow.

Sam linked her arm through his, and they headed for the door. A couple of times, she caught him staring at her out of the corner of his eye. *I hope Tom likes this dress as much as Marcus does.*

"What happened to Rachel?"

"She followed me to the bar and made a little dig about me losing my *girlfriend* so quickly, then she seemed to get bored and wandered off. She needs an audience.

"How did Darren get us into Omnia? I looked it up, and apparently, it's pretty hard to get on the list and very expensive."

"He's related to one of the big wigs, so he got us a comped table for eight with bottle service on the terrace. Those tables start at a thousand dollars, so we'll be styling tonight. He texted me that he'll be early. Have you heard from your friend?"

"No. I left him a message, but he hasn't answered. It's still early. You said the club doesn't open until 10:30, right?"

"Yeah, and if we enter with Darren, we won't have to worry about the line and the guest list."

Sam nodded and watched the sea of people surging around her. They seemed to be heading in all directions. "Are all these people waiting to get in?"

Marcus took another look. "No, that's the line there," He pointed at a wide swath of well-dressed people standing along one half of the sidewalk. "Everyone else is just out enjoying the strip."

Sam eyed the people in line and felt better about her outfit. Everyone was dressed to impress.

"We could go inside Caesar's and get a drink while we wait."

"Okay." She scanned the area. "I'll just text Tom again."

They entered the hotel and walked past the long line of people waiting to get inside Omnia when it opened. "I'm sure glad we don't have to wait in that line."

Marcus slung his arm around her shoulders again, so she looked at him. "What? It's comfortable. You're just the right height."

Sam laughed. "You're an odd duck."

"I know." He smirked.

They were just entering the lobby bar when Tom surprised Sam with a tap on her free shoulder.

"You're sneaky!" she said, smiling.

"Did you find another date?"

"No." Sam nudged Marcus' arm off her shoulders. "He's just messing with Rachel."

"Whew! Hello Marcus."

"Hello... um, what should I call you?"

"How about Tom while we're out and Detective when I'm on duty."

"Is it okay that you're out with us?"

"It's probably not a great idea, but just keep in mind that personal relationships won't change the outcome of the investigation, okay?"

"That sounds fair. We thought we'd get a drink while we waited."

Tom loosened his tie and took a closer look at Sam. "You look gorgeous."

Sam blushed and said, "Thank you. Marcus made me dress up." Then she laughed.

The waitress took their drinks order and disappeared.

Sam leaned toward Marcus and muttered, "I think we should tell him."

Marcus looked alarmed and shook his head violently.

"You two look like you need to discuss something. I'll just visit the men's room." Tom stood and strode away with purpose.

"Now I'm going to be afraid to leave the two of you alone together." He looked like he might be sick.

Sam wasn't paying attention to Marcus's pallor. She got distracted by the beautiful pink margarita the waitress placed in front of her. She took a sip. "I trust him, and if anything goes wrong tomorrow, it might be good to have him on standby."

He stiffened and took a gulp of his drink. "He's gonna want to play it by the book."

"He's out with a suspect tonight. He can always deny he knew anything."

"Sam, you understand how important this is to me. If he forbids us to do it or takes custody of the coins, I'm up the creek," Marcus nearly sobbed.

"Just let me feel him out. I won't tell him specifics, okay?"

"Promise me you won't screw this up for me."

She looked into his imploring eyes and finally noticed his physical distress. She put her hand on his. "I promise. Trust me."

"I do trust you." He mopped his forehead with his napkin. "I just don't know what I'll do if I don't get them back. I'm in a really bad spot."

"I'm in your corner. We'll figure something out, okay?"

He didn't look entirely convinced, but he nodded. "Hey! Here's Darren!" He relaxed perceptibly and grinned.

Darren grinned back as he approached. "I'm glad you could join us," he told Sam. I have a couple more friends coming too."

Sam recognized him from the Flamingo. He was the exact opposite of Marcus in looks and personality. Short and slim, blonde, spiky, surfer hair, and an easy-going demeanor. He had a way of making everyone around him feel comfortable. "Thanks so much for inviting us." Sam smiled.

"Any friend of Marcus is a friend of mine. I don't get comps like this all the time, so it's a special occasion." He waved for the waitress. "What are you drinking, Marcus?"

"Whiskey rocks."

The waitress returned, and Darren said, "I'll have what he's having," indicating Marcus with his thumb. Then he leaned back against Marcus's side and said, "What's going on?"

Tom returned, and Marcus said, "I'll tell you about it later. This is Sam's friend, Tom. Tom, this is Darren."

Tom reached across the table and shook Darren's hand. "Nice to meet you."

"You're a detective, right?"

"Yes. I've seen you at the Flamingo."

Darren smiled. "I'm there a lot." The waitress returned and handed him his drink.

"Thanks, Patty."

"Do you know everyone in Vegas?" Sam asked around her straw.

"Only the locals." His eyes twinkled merrily. "I grew up here, and it's a surprisingly small world."

"Plus, everyone loves you. They can't help it," Marcus said fondly.

Sam felt warm and fuzzy seeing them so happy together. She looked at Tom with soft eyes and smiled when she saw him watching her.

Once they had finished their drinks, Darren said, "It's just about opening time. Is everyone ready?"

They all stood and prepared to leave for Omnia.

Darren ushered them through the VIP line and upstairs to a large, cordoned-off booth overlooking the strip.

Tom took Sam's elbow and watched her as she soaked up the ambiance. More and more people crowded into the noisy venue until hundreds of bodies bobbed up and down, and hundreds of arms reached into the air. Sam's dress seemed to take on a life of its own as the flashing lights hit the silver sequins.

Upstairs, they got comfortable in their booth and met Darren's friends.

"Randy and Karen are old friends from school. They have a baby at home, so they don't get out much." Darren winked at Karen.

She smiled and said, "This is such a treat. I'm so happy you invited us." She elbowed Randy.

"Oof! Happy wife, happy life, right?" He laughed.

"I work with Bob and Ron. Sort of."

"They separate us, so we don't have too much fun," Ron took a drink.

"Oh, you!" Bob swatted him on the shoulder. "They separate us because there are a lot of bars and not enough bartenders."

"Says you. It's time for fun now. Have a drink, and then we'll boogie."

"Why don't we dance, Sam?" Tom stood and took her hand.

She stood and gave a little wave to the others, then let Tom lead her into the throng on the dance floor.

He couldn't take his eyes off her. The transformation from casual girl next door to supermodel was breathtaking. He felt self-conscious on the dance floor at first, but Sam put him at ease. He followed her individual brand of dancing and stopped worrying about what anyone else was thinking. When a slow song began playing, he pulled her close and felt his heart thrumming to the music.

"This is nice. What did you think you should tell me?"

"I don't want to put you in a hard place, but I think you should know."

He nuzzled her ear and waited.

"No, I can't think straight when we're so close."

Tom chuckled. "I apologize, but I'm not very sorry."

"It's lovely dancing with you. My brain just seems to have shut down." Sam's lips turned upward.

He wanted to kiss her, but he didn't.

When the song ended, they returned to the table and found it empty. They slid into the booth and poured themselves drinks. He ran a finger slowly down her arm. "Is your brain working now?" Tom's eyes twinkled when she shivered.

"Umm. Not sure. But Cathy asked me to go with her to revisit the places we went the morning Roy died. We're planning to go at noon tomorrow. It might be nothing, but Marcus told me I should let you know."

"I'll be on standby in case you need me." He smiled at her.

Marcus and Darren returned to the table, glistening. "Are we interrupting?" Marcus asked.

Tom shook his head and said, "Sam told me about tomorrow, and I told her I'd be on standby." He didn't notice Sam surreptitiously shake her head. "I don't think Cathy's a killer, but she is a suspect."

Marcus' eyebrows rose slightly. "Can't be too careful."

The others returned as well, but Sam couldn't remember their names. After several drinks, she was mesmerized by Tom's eyes.

The Cardinal, The Fat Boy & The Flamingo

Gazing into their depths is like laying in the grass and watching the clouds. They are constantly changing with his thoughts.

"Sam, are you okay?" she heard him ask.

"Yes, I'm fine. We should dance some more."

They danced for quite some time, which, along with some hors d' oeuvres, helped Sam sober up considerably. When they returned to the table, she said, "I suppose we should call it a night. We have a busy day tomorrow. Thank you again, Darren. This was an amazing experience."

Darren nodded but quickly returned his attention to Marcus. Tom took Sam's arm and guided her through the wall of partiers. "What do you do after I see you back to the hotel? Do you slip off to the casino?"

"No, I actually go to sleep. What time do you get up?"

"Somewhere between four and five. If Harvey got in before me, he'd probably faint."

Sam laughed. "Four o'clock is too early. Six might be okay."

"I don't ordinarily have much to do outside my work. Trying to keep up with you is making me rethink my hours."

"Ranch hours usually coincide with daylight hours, so there's never been a reason for me to rise before the birds."

"I'd like to see your ranch someday."

"I'd like that too."

They arrived back at the Flamingo, and Tom hesitated. "Would you like me to walk you to your room?"

"No, that's okay. Thanks for going with me tonight."

He leaned in to kiss her, but she turned to give him her cheek. *I like him so much, but it's pointless. I could never give up the ranch.* Sam smiled sadly. "Goodnight, Tom."

Chapter 11

Sam went up to her room, looked up the closest Catholic church, and found one in old downtown that had mass every morning at nine. She needed to be grounded in her faith, to talk to God.

She changed into her pajamas and knelt at her bedside.

Father, I have met someone I really like, and I don't know why it always has to be so complicated. I danced with him tonight, and it was magic, but I can't live here. I was raised on the ranch; it's where I belong. This town is fun for a few days, but I need to go home. I don't want my time with him to be meaningless and leave us both hurt, so it's best not to get too attached, isn't it? The temptation is there. Just see where it goes. But I am so afraid of being hurt again. Please guide me, Lord. Show me how to proceed. In the name of the Father, the Son, and the Holy Ghost. Amen.

Sam crossed herself and got into bed. She closed her eyes and dreamt of a flamingo with piercing blue eyes.

The following morning, Sam felt exhausted, but she had made plans to meet Marcus at the coffee shop at nine. He looked as tired as she felt. "Late night?" she asked.

"Yeah." He grinned. "You too, I guess."

"No, I just didn't sleep well."

"That's because you sent him home. Why did you change your mind about sharing our plan?"

"It wouldn't be fair. He couldn't possibly be okay with it."

"True. We're still on?"

Sam nodded.

"We'll head up at 10:15. I have a borrowed keycard.

You can keep an eye on the door, and I'll work my magic on the safe. If anyone comes, let me know, and we'll hide in the bedroom closet. If no one comes, I'll look through the stuff in the safe and see if the coins are there."

"What if they aren't?"

"If we have time, I'll search the rest of the suite. If time is short, then we'll leave."

The idea didn't sound very well thought out to Sam, but she had agreed to help him, so she was in.

They left the coffee shop at ten and headed for the stairs instead of the elevator. They were both out of breath by the time they reached Greg and Lizzie's floor, so they rested a moment before Marcus peeked out of the stairwell. He saw Lizzie boarding the elevator. They waited a few minutes, then Marcus led the way to the room. Everything went according to plan until Greg stepped off the elevator at 10:45. Sam flew across the room and grabbed Marcus. "Closet. Now!" She whispered.

They ran for the closet, and both tried to get through the narrow door at the same time. "Ow! You just stomped on my foot."

"Shhh! Augh! Cramp!" Sam bent to rub out the cramp in her calf and hit Marcus' solar plexus with her head. He doubled over, wheezing, and got smacked in the head when she straightened.

Holding his head, Marcus said, "I think it might be safer out there with him."

The closet door jerked open, and the two of them tumbled out onto the floor. Sam looked up to see Greg holding a gun and looking like a storm cloud.

"Just what do you two think you're doing in my room?"

Silence.

"Well?"

"Just tell him, Marcus."

Marcus rolled onto his knees. "Can we get up off the floor?"

"No! Stay right where you are." Greg waved his gun around.

Marcus sighed. "I don't know where to begin."

"Marcus invested everything he had into Roy's business," Sam began.

Greg just stared at her.

"When Roy was killed, his safe was open and empty. Marcus thought that either the murderer took the assets or that Roy might have given them to you for safe keeping."

Greg took a step back and glared at Marcus. "Why didn't you just ask me?"

"Because that would be dangerous if you were the murderer."

"If I found you in my room, that could also be dangerous. And why bring *her*?"

"She was supposed to be my lookout and a witness that I didn't take anything that wasn't mine."

Greg crossed his arms and tapped his foot. "I wouldn't give up my day job for a life of crime if I were you. Come into the living room."

Once they were seated, Greg poured them each a shot of bourbon. "You're right. Roy documented everything and asked me to hold onto them."

"Thank god!" Marcus put his hand on his chest. "Maybe we can still go to the show and sell them."

"Did you invest too?" Sam asked Greg.

"Something like that."

Sam put her hands up. "Not my business. I get it."

"Don't go yapping to your boyfriend," Greg said.

"Unless it has something to do with the murder, I don't have any interest in your business."

"Good." He put his gun down.

Sam tilted her head to the side. "Why do you think he asked you to hold the coins?"

"He was thinking about divorce and didn't want Cathy to take them. She had access to their safe."

"Divorce? After they had sold their home? Did anyone else know about that?"

"Just Lizzie. She overheard their argument."

Sam's mouth made an oh. "Why did he want a divorce?"

"She was very jealous and kept accusing him of having affairs."

"Was he?"

He paced back and forth and scratched the bald spot on the top of his head. "I think he might have given in to Rachel once or twice. I'm not sure."

"Do you think she might have killed him?"

Greg shook his head. "Cathy? Nah. I don't think she has it in her."

"What kind of gun did he have?"

"A nine-millimeter, I think."

"Don't mention that to anyone else, okay?"

"Sure."

"I'm heading out. Glad you two got the coins sorted."

Sam went back to her room and got into her swimsuit. She had plenty of time, so she headed for the pool. She chose the family pool and floated around, lost in thought. *If my partner had sold our house and maintained a secret business... if he had control over all our money... if he was talking about divorcing me... how would I feel? I think I would panic. To be fifty years old and completely dependent on someone I couldn't trust. That would be terrifying. Would I think I needed to protect myself? How would I go about doing that? Could Cathy have committed murder?*

Sam was so caught up in her train of thought that Cal startled her when he touched her shoulder.

"Augh!" she shouted, arms and legs flailing.

"Sorry. You were really off in your own world there."

Hands on her knees, Sam took a minute to let her breathing and heart rate slow to normal. "Jeez. You'll give someone a heart attack doing that."

"Sorry." He looked contrite.

"What's up?"

85

"Nothing, really. We were all just talking about taking a little road trip day after tomorrow, and I wanted to invite you. We haven't been out on our bikes at all since last week."

"That would be great! Can I bring a friend?"

"I don't see why not. We'll meet out front at two and find somewhere to eat along the way."

Sam smiled. "Thanks, Cal. That will be fun! What time is it now?"

"It's noon."

"I have to meet Cathy at 12:30, so I'd better run." She waded to the side of the pool and grabbed her towel.

Once inside, she showered and dressed, placing a call to Tom as she got ready.

Sam was a little nervous, but she didn't really believe that Cathy had anything to do with Roy's death. Mostly Sam was worried that she might say or do the wrong thing. *I don't want to accidentally make her feel worse when she's working so hard to heal.* Sam spotted her when she exited the elevator and strode over to where she was waiting.

"Hi, Cathy! Ready for our excursion?"

"Oh! There you are, dear. I'm ready."

"You lead the way since I'm not sure I remember exactly. We saw so many things."

"Yes, we did. I know we started off on the Linq Promenade, so let's get there first."

They walked through the crush of tourists, and Sam remembered the uncomfortable, claustrophobic feeling of passing through the entrance to the promenade. "I heard that there's a lot of theft in this area."

"Yes, watch your things," Cathy said distractedly.

They stopped in the stores they had visited the previous Sunday and a few new ones. Cathy even stopped in the same restrooms. They ate ice cream by the fountain and rode the *High Roller*.

Finally, they stopped at In 'N Out for burgers and animal fries, but Cathy didn't ask for the same order to go. Sam noticed but didn't comment.

"This is where I'll break the cycle, dear. I'll walk back by myself and go to my new room."

Sam nodded and looked away as an errant tear threatened to fall. "Thank you for including me today, Cathy."

They stood, and Sam gave her a half hug, then watched her walk away, clutching her purse close to her body. She called Tom. "Cathy's walking back alone. Do you want me to follow her?"

"No, you finish those fries."

Sam stared at her fries on the table. "Where are you?"

"Inside the restaurant, getting us milkshakes." He laughed and disconnected the call, arriving at the table seconds later.

"You're sneaky!" Sam's eyes sparkled.

"Maybe. Chocolate or vanilla?"

"Chocolate, of course."

"I had a suspicion you would say that. Did you learn anything?"

"Not really. Want some fries?"

"I was hoping you'd ask." He grabbed a fry and stuck it in his mouth.

She leaned closer and whispered, "I'll tell you a secret. I don't really love these animal fries. I would rather have them plain."

Tom leaned toward her and whispered, "Me too."

They both leaned back and laughed.

Chapter 12

Sam avoided everyone the next morning. She ordered room service for breakfast, then took off on her Fat Boy to find the cathedral. The ride took her almost half an hour, and when she pulled into the parking lot, her eyes widened at the immensity of the stone building. The inside was grander than any church she had ever seen. Sam didn't spend much time exploring, but she noticed a lot of art, a huge social hall, and even a gift store. *I'll come back and look around another time.* The sanctuary was rapidly filling, so she hurried to take her seat.

The bishop gave a sermon about marriage, focusing on 2 Corinthians 6:14. "Do not be unequally yoked with unbelievers. For what partnership has righteousness with lawlessness? Or what fellowship has light with darkness?" He spoke of waiting for God to bring the right person into your life, and Sam felt like his sermon was just for her. She listened carefully and took this message to heart, feeling grateful that God had spoken to her that morning.

Back at the Flamingo, Sam spent some time at the pool, floating around peacefully. Raised voices drew her attention. Rachel and Cal were having an intense looking discussion under the waterfall feature. Cal had a stony face and clenched his fists as Rachel spoke with her face very close to his. *That would bother me a lot. I wonder what they're talking about.* Suddenly Rachel gave Cal a shove, knocking him into the pool, and strode out of the pool area.

Pedro walked over to Cal, laughing, and helped him out of the pool. Cal shook himself like a dog and flung his arms around as he spoke rapidly.

Marcus tapped Sam on the shoulder, startling her. "I wonder what that was about."

"I wonder why they dislike each other so much," she said.

"It's odd. Want to get some lunch? I heard something interesting this morning."

"Okay. The little place upstairs?"

They grabbed a couple of towels, and Sam said suddenly, "Do you have any family besides Cathy?"

Marcus gave her an odd look. "Cathy isn't family. I never even met her before I came here."

"Most people think of aunts and uncles as part of their family, I think. But you didn't answer my question."

"No, I don't have any family. My mom and dad died, and I was an only child. That's why I was so excited when Uncle Roy asked me to join Torque."

"I don't have any family either, except my cousin Jack, who I found out isn't really my cousin." Sam paused. "Maybe we can be honorary family, you and I."

Marcus smiled and slung his arm over her shoulders again. "Cousins or siblings?"

"Siblings, for sure." Sam nodded.

"I'm in, but since I'm older, you have to do everything I tell you to."

"Not a chance." She bumped her hip against his. "You can't be much older, anyway."

"I'm 35."

"Really? I would never have guessed it. Mom and dad must have gotten a second wind. You're ten years older than I am."

They arrived at the Beach Club and sat at a table with a view of the pool area. Deciding on beef sliders and fries, Marcus leaned in after the waitress left and said, "I overheard that Lizzy isn't who she claims to be. Apparently, she's from some rich and famous family, and she's hiding her identity."

"I don't know. He shrugged. Maybe it doesn't have anything to do with the investigation."

"Are you going to dinner tonight?"

He put his hands around his throat and made a face. "I suppose I must. It's a little like a train wreck, isn't it?"

Sam nodded. "I know what you mean. It's usually painful, but I don't want to miss anything."

"You know it's your turn to pick, right?"

Sam stared at him. "Pick?"

"Yeah. We take turns picking the restaurant. So, you should probably decide."

"A little warning might be nice. Sheesh."

Cathy and Dani walked through the shops in the Venetian hotel that afternoon. Cathy enjoyed the beautiful blue sky painted high above their heads and the gondolas gliding along the canal. It was peaceful if you could block out the noise. "Would it be okay if we sit down for a few minutes, dear? I'm feeling a little tired."

"Sure. I could find us something to drink if you want."

"Thank you." Cathy smiled as she watched Dani sashay toward the nearest vendor, then she turned her attention back to the water. *I've always loved the water. I wonder if I have enough money to move back to Florida. I should have told Roy I wanted to go home.*

"Here you go," Dani said, surprising her. "I didn't ask what kind of drink you wanted, but I figured we could both use some water." She handed Cathy a bottle of water, then gaped toward the canal. "Would you look at that? Greg and Lizzie are in that gondola!"

Cathy turned back to the water and saw her friends. She waved, but they were deep in conversation and didn't notice her.

"I wish Pedro did romantic stuff like that." Dani pouted. "All he's ever interested in are his stupid motorcycles."

Cathy patted her hand. "Perhaps he just needs the right incentive." Her mind drifted back to the days when she and Roy were young and the silly things she did to get his attention.

She smiled at the memories and blinked the moisture from her eyes. *I sure do miss him.*

Dani sat down on the bench next to Cathy. "I'm sorry. I am so inconsiderate. Do you want to go on a gondola ride? We could go, just you and me."

"No, I'm happy just watching the boats gliding along in the water. They're very peaceful." She looked at Dani's shopping bags. "What do you do with all of the things you buy? Do you mail them home?"

Dani laughed. "I've been telling Pedro he needs to get bigger saddlebags. What do you think Greg and Lizzie are talking about?"

Cathy noticed Dani didn't answer. She looked around at all the shoppers. *I wonder what I would do with my things if I kept buying new clothes all the time.*

Dani put her hand on her shoulder. "Cathy? Are you okay?"

"I have no idea. Maybe they're talking about whether or not to continue with *Torque.* Have you and Pedro discussed it?"

"No." Dani shook her head. "He never asks for my opinion. I don't know what he'd do if I put my foot down. So far, I haven't really cared one way or the other."

"Maybe we should have a meeting and talk about it. I don't think I'll continue without Roy. This was his dream, not mine."

"It just won't be the same without you," Dani whined.

"I know. I'll miss you too. Maybe we could all find a large house to live in and take road trips together whenever we like."

Dani's eyes got round. "Like a mansion? Wouldn't that be grand? We could send the men out on road trips, and we could stay home and eat cake." She laughed.

"We'd have to have a pool, of course," Cathy continued with their theme.

"And lots of fruit trees."

"It sounds so lovely." She paused. "Anyway, we should probably have a meeting. Maybe after our road trip tomorrow."

"Where are we going, anyway?"

"Valley of Fire, it's called. I've never been there, but it's supposed to be gorgeous."

"It sounds hot. I hate sweating in leather pants."

"Maybe you could wear something else."

"No way. If I'm going to be a motorcycle chick, then by god, I'll look like one!"

Cathy laughed. "I do get a kick out of you, Dani. Why don't we head back to the hotel so we can get ready for dinner?"

"Where are we eating tonight?"

"I don't know, actually." Cathy looked at her phone. "Sam sent a group text. Blackout at seven."

Chapter 13

Detectives Cork and Brother spent that Thursday comparing evidence and looking into suspect backgrounds. They entered the Flamingo and approached the front desk. The staff had been instructed to cooperate.

"Good afternoon, detectives."

"Hello," Tom squinted at his name tag, "Grant. Have you seen anyone from *Torque* recently?"

"I think several of them might be at the pool."

"Great. Thank you."

Tom turned to Harvey and said, "Do you know where the pool is?"

"I do. Right this way."

They showed their badges to get in, then scanned the pool. "Cal is first on the list."

"There he is." Harvey pointed.

Tom watched Cal as he made his way to the edge of the pool and grabbed a towel. *He can't seem to walk three feet without harassing any female in sight. He must be really annoying.* Cal slowly dried the water off his limbs, looking around to see if anyone was admiring him. Tom shook his head.

Harvey began to walk toward Cal. When they got close enough, Tom said, "Excuse me, Mr. Lenox, could we have just a moment? I have a couple additional questions."

Cal rolled his eyes and bounced on his toes. "Yes, what is it? I'd like to get changed."

"Well, you said you didn't see anyone else between ten and one on the day Roy died."

"Yeah. So?" Call crossed his arms.

"Someone told us they stopped and talked to you that morning."

"They must be lying."

"We also found an unregistered firearm and a container of Ecstasy in your room."

Cal's face turned an unpleasant shade of purple. "What? You have no right to be in my room!"

"We did have a warrant and left a message for you regarding the date and time."

"Someone gave them to me for safekeeping. They weren't mine."

Tom rubbed his chin but said nothing.

"Refusing to give a complete and accurate statement of your whereabouts makes us question any other statements you make," Harvey explained.

"Thank you for your time," Tom said as he turned and walked off.

Harvey hurried to catch up. "Who told you they talked to him in the hallway?"

"No one. I saw it on the video footage."

They found Greg and Lizzie in the bar. "Why don't you take the lead on this one, Harve?" Tom gave him a nudge and followed him in.

"Excuse me, sir. We'd like to ask you a few more questions about the morning of Mr. Williams' murder."

"Of course." Greg stood.

"You said that neither you nor your wife left the bar that morning, but we have a witness who said both of you left at some point."

"I did go to the restroom," Lizzie volunteered. "Then I ran into Cal in the hallway. He wouldn't stop talking, as usual, so I might have been a while."

"She did leave, but I did not. If you ask the bartender, he can verify that."

"Thank you. Also, you told us your gun had disappeared, but when we searched your room, we found it."

Greg grimaced. "I didn't want you to confiscate it and possibly put Lizzie in danger."

"It has been taken in for testing now since the murder weapon was also a 9mm," Harvey said.

"I understand."

"Mrs. Scott," Tom said, "could I have a word in private?"

She stepped back and frowned, looking at her husband.

"I'm sure it's fine, dear," Greg assured her. "Go ahead."

Lizzie and Tom sat at a table out of earshot. Gently and quietly, he asked, "Why are you using a false identity?"

She stared at him for a moment, then shivered. "Some of the people in my family are bad. I was kept in a mansion with security guards all around me until I was almost thirty. I ran away and met Greg. He helped me become someone else."

Tom carefully covered his surprise. "Is that what Cal was talking to you about?"

"Yes. He wants money. I haven't told Greg because I'm worried about what he might do." Lizzie's forehead wrinkled, and she clasped her hands. "He's a good man, but he's also very protective."

Tom pressed his lips together. "I'll try to take care of Cal."

"You won't tell anyone?"

"As long as it doesn't have anything to do with the murder."

"It doesn't. I swear it. Roy was Greg's best friend." Lizzie looked sadly at Tom with tears in her eyes. "Nothing will ever be the same now."

"Thank you for your honesty."

Lizzie nodded and stood. She walked shakily back to Greg, who spoke in her ear and hugged her.

Tom and Harvey left the bar and headed for the elevators again.

"This is clearing up some loose ends, sir. But is it helping us solve the case?"

"Yes, I believe so, Harvey. Let's go find Sam."

Tom knocked on Sam's door and was amused when she answered it with her short, spiky hair going in every direction.

"Hello, detectives. How can I help you?"

"May we come in and talk to you for a moment?"

"Of course! Come on in and sit at the table. Would you like some water?"

"Yes, please."

Sam gave each of them a bottle and took one for herself. "I got them at CVS. The prices here are highway robbery!"

"You learn fast." Harvey smiled.

"Have you found out anything new today?" Tom asked.

"Yes. Sort of. I saw Cal and Rachel arguing. She seemed very angry and shoved him into the pool."

"More blackmail, perhaps," Tom muttered.

"Also, I found out we take turns picking where we eat dinner, and tonight is my turn. We're eating at Blackout. Want to join us?"

"It wouldn't be much fun if I couldn't see you." Tom grinned, and Harvey looked away. "We can still meet for breakfast, and you can tell me more about the road trip tomorrow."

"Sounds good. Where are we eating?"

"It's a surprise. I'll pick you up on my bike. Is seven too early?"

"No, that's fine."

"See you then." Tom smiled. He and Harvey rose and headed for the door. He looked back at her as they left and caught her soft look when her face was relaxed and her eyes shuttered just a bit. It gave him courage for what he wanted to say to her at breakfast.

96

Chapter 14

Sam met the rest of *Torque* at Blackout. She and Marcus had chosen the thirty-minute walk, so they didn't have to worry about drinking and driving. *It might also be a good idea to walk off some of that food when we're done.* The restaurant was unique because diners ate unidentified dishes in the dark to enhance their other senses. *It probably wouldn't be a good choice for a picky eater. It might or might not help the strained atmosphere between the members.*

The staff at the door asked some simple questions about likes and dislikes and dietary requirements, then led the entire group, through the darkness, to their table. Cathy was behind Sam, with her hand on Sam's shoulder. Sam was behind Marcus with her hand on his shoulder. She couldn't even see her hand. It was impossible to tell whether the restaurant was big or small and whether it was crowded or not. It was noisy, but that might have been a symptom of the darkness; people talked louder because they didn't know where the person they were talking to was located. Once seated, the server asked each of them to choose a flavor palette. Sam chose the spicy palette. She felt unnerved at first by the sound of voices around her in the dark. She could hear the rustling of clothing, footsteps, and chewing.

Their dinner consisted of seven courses, all vegan. The first course was brought out, and everyone began to guess what it was. Sam smelled coconut but couldn't identify what she was eating.

"Marcus? Do we have the same dish?"

"I don't know. Take my fork and try it." Sam found his elbow and worked her way down to his hand.

"It's really strange not being able to see even an outline."

She took his fork and had a taste of his food. "It's the same food, I think, but a different flavor. Mine's supposed to be spicy."

"Rachel's having a panic attack," Cathy said. "Where's that emergency button?"

"There's one here," Marcus said. He felt around for a moment, then pushed the button.

The waiter arrived and helped Rachel out of the dining area.

"I would have to leave too if Greg wasn't here," Lizzie's disembodied voice floated down the table.

Sam gave up on the first course. She couldn't identify what it was and thought it was kind of mushy. When the second course came, she could smell tarragon and dill. She took a bite and was pleasantly surprised by the pungent taste and smell. "This one has garbanzo beans in it and red peppers. I'm not sure what I'd call it, but at least I can recognize some of the ingredients."

"I don't like this pretend food," Pedro commented. "I need some meat."

"It's pretty good, and maybe it's healthy. We could use some healthy food," Dani said.

"Speak for yourself."

"Is Cal still here?" Cathy asked.

Sam looked around, even though she couldn't see anything.

"Cal?" Pedro said.

"I'm here," he said faintly. "I'm not feeling too good."

"Hit the button again, Marcus," Greg said.

Maybe this wasn't such a great idea. The waiter came with the third course and led Cal from the dining room. The third course was some kind of pasta.

"My pasta has shrimp in it. Isn't this supposed to be a vegan restaurant?"

"It's fake shrimp, Lizzie," Greg said.

"That's not fair. I didn't tell them I don't like seafood because I thought it wouldn't be an issue."

Sam leaned toward Marcus's chair and whispered, "I think I could use another drink."

"Now that's a good idea."

The fourth course arrived, and everyone ordered drinks.

"Salad?" Pedro said loudly.

Sam put her hand over her mouth so he wouldn't hear her laugh, then she took a bite of her salad. *It's the best so far. It's tart and crunchy; a good palate cleanser.*

Sam savored each course, noting the different flavors and textures. *This would be a fun thing to do with Jack. I should call him.* Her companions were so busy eating and talking about their dinner they were too busy to fight. When they finally reached dessert, Sam felt tired. The sensory overload and the rich food made her feel like taking a nap.

After dinner, everyone was still talking about the experience, and they decided to stop by *Ghost Donkey* for cocktails.

"Do we have to go?" she asked Marcus.

"No, but it will be an experience. Let's just go see what the hype is about, then we can leave."

The Cosmopolitan Hotel, where it was located, wasn't far from the Flamingo, so Sam agreed. The others had taken their bikes to dinner, and Marcus suggested they could call an Uber, but Sam wanted to walk.

"That meal made me sleepy. A walk will help clear my head."

Marcus shrugged. "I don't mind."

"What did you do before you joined *Torque?*" Sam asked as they walked.

"My parents owned a catering company. I worked there for a long time, learning each position from the ground up. I was supposed to take over the business when my father retired, but he died before I could finish my training. I guess I could have kept it open and tried to learn as I went, but I was mourning and just didn't have it in me.

So I closed the business and went to bar-tending school." He looked at Sam.

"I get it." She nodded. "The ranch was a family business too. I might have done the same thing if it wasn't also my home. Look. There's the Cosmopolitan."

Marcus looked in the direction she was pointing. "Let's go find that donkey."

One of the draws for the *Ghost Donkey* was its status as a secret, *hidden* bar. They had to search deep within the hotel to find it, in the back of the block 16 food court, with nothing but a picture of a donkey on a door marked as an exit. When Marcus opened the door, they were transported into a small speakeasy. Hundreds of tiny lights twinkled overhead, and the crush of people bobbed to lively music. Cathy was holding court on a cozy sofa lining the back of the room.

"This is great." Sam grinned. "Look at those nachos!"

"Are you still hungry?"

"I'm always hungry."

Unfortunately, Pedro was a mean drunk, and he'd consumed his fair share of tequila by the time Sam and Marcus arrived. He and Cal were toe to toe, having a heated argument, and Dani was ready to leave.

"I wonder what they're arguing about," Marcus said.

"See if you can find out, and I'll go get us drinks."

Marcus moved a little closer but was waylaid by Dani. "Will you dance with me? Pedro's snockered. He didn't eat much and can't ever say no to shots of tequila."

"I don't want to piss off a snockered Pedro. Why's he mad at Cal? I thought they were friends."

"I don't know. Something about a job. Cal thinks they should lay off for a while because the cops are sniffing around."

"He could have a point."

100

"Yeah, but I guess something really good has come up."

Marcus shrugged and took the drink Sam handed him when she got back. "Maybe the two of you should dance. Pedro can't get too mad about that."

"Very funny." Dani stuck her tongue out. "I'll just have to find a brave stranger."

Marcus and Sam watched her walk away. "She's playing with fire," he said.

Pedro and Cal started swinging their fists, and they were escorted from the hotel, so everyone decided to call it a night. By the time security dragged them outside, the two men had calmed down. Pedro stumbled and flung his arm around Cal's shoulders, almost knocking them both over. He took a deep breath and began belting out the lyrics to an old Mexican song. He tried to add a little dance step but stumbled again.

"Ay, no!" Dani exclaimed.

"Estoy desapareciendo en el rio," Pedro slurred off key.

"Is he singing?" Marcus asked.

"De humanidad vacio."

"Stop it, you drunken fool!"

Pedro turned and walked up to Dani, putting his face close to hers and singing the last line quietly, "Ya no me importas querida," before rejoining Cal.

Dani tried to shrug it off, but she was quiet the rest of the walk back.

"What just happened?" Marcus asked.

"It's a Mexican song. The last line he sang was you're not important to me anymore."

"Yikes. Was he breaking up with her?"

Sam shrugged. "I think he was just singing, but then again, I don't really know him." She turned and looked behind them. "Where's Cathy?"

"She, Greg, and Lizzie are back a ways. I saw them coming down the escalator as we left."

"It's too bad we had to leave so soon. I didn't get my nachos."

"Maybe we can go back sometime."

After she had said goodnight and was back in her room, Sam thought back to Pedro's song. Dani had been pretty aggressive. Was Pedro warning her? Were the lyrics just a coincidence? *It's none of my business, but still… there's a lot I don't know about this group.*

Sam was very tired after her long day, and she kept dozing off while she was trying to pray. She felt guilty for not being able to focus but finally said, "Thank you, Lord. Please forgive me," and went to bed. She was asleep almost before her head hit the pillow.

Chapter 15

The next morning, Tom was waiting out front when Sam came downstairs. She walked around his bike, admiring the sleek lines and running her hand along the shiny black paint. "It's beautiful," she breathed.

"Good morning to you too." He chuckled. "Ready to go?"

"Sorry! Good morning!" She hopped on behind him and put her helmet on.

"I hope you have an appetite this morning."

Sam wrapped her arms around his waist as he revved his engine. "You will find that I almost always have an appetite."

Tom laughed and took off down the street. Ten minutes later, he pulled up to Siegel's Bagelmania, helped Sam off the bike, and said, "We have arrived!"

Sam gawked at the huge turquoise and white building and the giant bagel on the sign. "Everything in Las Vegas is so big!"

Tom enjoyed her first impressions. "Be prepared for a giant sandwich as well."

Inside, they found glass cases filled with rows and rows of donuts, pastries, bagels, meats, and cheeses. Tom watched Sam as she looked around before focusing on the menu. "What are you having?"

Tom thought for a moment. "I'll have the Wake & Bake. Do you like chorizo?"

Sam tilted her head and looked at him with wide eyes. "Of course."

"The Spicy Feinstein is good. We could swap half so you can try both."

"Good idea!"

They placed their orders and sat at one of the many spread-out tables. "This is nice and relaxed after all of the lights and noise on the Strip," Sam said.

"The noise gets to me too."

Their bagel sandwiches were ready in about ten minutes, and Tom laughed at the incredulous expression on Sam's face when she saw them.

She gave him half of her sandwich, then looked inside. "Chorizo, pico de gallo, avocado & charred jalapeño schmear stacked with two fried eggs & hash brown cake."

Tom handed her half of his in return. His bagel was filled with nova and baked salmon salad, tomato, cucumber, red onion, and chive schmear.

"Which one is better?"

"Why don't you take a bite of each? Then you can decide."

Sam pretended to pout.

"Fine. If you like salmon, the sandwich I ordered is the best I have ever eaten anywhere. It might make you swoon."

Sam's lips formed an oh. She picked up the other sandwich to take a bite.

"You don't believe me?"

"No, I do. I want to leave the best for last."

"Tell me about tomorrow's road trip," Tom said between bites.

"We're supposed to ride to the Valley of Fire, then get something to eat on the way back."

"Can you take a tracker with you?"

Sam was busy chewing, so she just nodded.

"I can follow a ways behind, and you can call me if anything happens. Just try not to be alone with anyone, okay?"

Sam shrugged. "I trust Marcus. I think I'll be okay if we stick together."

Tom frowned. "Just be careful. What are you doing?"

Sam had one large bite of sandwich left, sitting in the middle of her plate. She was staring at it intently. "I don't want it to end." She picked it up and stuck it in her mouth, chewing slowly with a blissful expression on her face.

When they were finished, there wasn't a crumb left on either of their plates. Sam leaned back and put her hands on her flat stomach. "Both of those sandwiches were fantastic! Ten out of ten would recommend a friend! Wooo! I'm stuffed."

"I was wondering where you were putting all of that. Which one did you like best?"

"You were right, of course. The Wake & Bake was incredible! Let's try the root beer floats now!"

"You're kidding, right?"

The fake pout reappeared.

"Root beer floats it is." He laughed and shook his head on the way to the counter. When he returned to the table, Sam said, "I don't know how much time you have, but I was wondering if you would go to mass with me this morning."

"I'm afraid I have to get back to the station. Some other time maybe?"

Sam was disappointed, but she said, "Sure. I know you're supposed to be working."

Tom knew he had failed a test, and his courage flagged. He would have to tell her another time.

After breakfast, Tom drove Sam back to the Flamingo. He gave her a brief kiss, reminded her to be careful, and took off on his bike.

Pedro caught up with Sam as she crossed the lobby and walked with her to the elevator. "You're pretty tight with that detective, huh?"

"We're friends, I think."

"Did he tell you about Dani's alibi?"

"No. Why?"

105

"She won't tell me what she was up to."

Sam raised her brows in question. "Do you think she killed Roy?"

"No way! I just don't like her sneaking around."

Sam shrugged and poked the call button.

"Did you tell the detective about my business?"

The elevator doors slid open, and they got on. "The repair shop?"

"Dani told me you heard her and Marcus talking."

"Did she also tell you that I don't care about your shop unless it has something to do with the murder?"

"No... she left that part out. So, you didn't tell him?"

"No. Still not my business."

Pedro nodded as the doors opened again. "Thanks. Sorry if I've been a jerk," he mumbled.

"No problem. See you this afternoon." *These people. What a messed up bunch.* Sam decided to have a swim, then take a rest. She had water and snacks to take along, but the trip would be hot and tiring.

Chapter 16

Despite the heat, Sam was in high spirits as *Torque* left Las Vegas in formation. Greg and Pedro led the way, with Lizzie and Dani in their passenger seats. The desert heat was oppressive, even in jeans and a long-sleeved t-shirt. *Lizzie and Dani must be dying in those leathers.* Cathy and Rachel followed behind, then Cal. Marcus and Sam brought up the rear. She had caught sight of Cathy's face before she put on her helmet and worried that this might be too soon. Cal and Rachel had also seemed subdued after the night before.

The hour-long ride was unimpressive for someone who had grown up in the southwest. Flat expanses of dry desert scrub could be seen for miles in every direction. Sam's pulse quickened, however, as large rock formations appeared in the distance. She researched Valley of Fire State Park before they left the hotel. She saw pictures of large, intricate sandstone formations in myriad shades of red, formed 150 million years ago by shifting sand. Her excitement was palpable; she wanted to drive faster. Unfortunately, Greg was cruising along at exactly the speed limit. Sam had never driven with a group before but assumed it would be bad manners to race ahead.

When they finally entered the park and paid their entrance fees, their first destination was the *Beehives* on the left. Instead, they drove right by it and onto Campground road. Pulling over at *Atlatl Rock*, Greg removed his helmet and announced that there were restrooms there. Sam wanted to explore everything, but first things first. She took a long drink of water, then peeled off her long-sleeved t-shirt. She pulled her shorts and sunscreen out of her saddlebags and raced for the restrooms. *It's still hot, but that's so much better!*

Dani was in one of the stalls. "These damn pants are stuck to me!" she screeched. "Why do we have to be out here in this heat?"

"I have some baby powder," Lizzie said from another stall.

Sam left the restroom because she didn't want them to see her in her shorts. She sprayed on her sunscreen in the shade, then walked by Cal on her way back. "Would you like to borrow some sunscreen?"

"I don't use that stuff," he boasted.

"The sun can roast you out here. It wouldn't hurt."

"I've never used it. Never will!"

Marcus approached, and they watched Cal stomp away. "What's up with him?"

"He was insulted that I offered him sunscreen."

Marcus raised his eyebrows. "Can I use some?"

Sam handed him the can. "I want to get my hat and sunglasses." She walked back to her bike, put her clothes in her saddlebags, then retrieved her hat, glasses, and water. "Ready to explore the rock?"

Marcus handed her the sunscreen. "Yes, ma'am. And thanks for this."

"I rarely burn," Sam said, "but the sun out here is harsh." She looked up at *Atlatl Rock* with her mouth open. "Would you look at that crazy huge rock? I read there are petroglyphs up there."

"Let's get climbing then."

Sam didn't count the steps, but there were a lot of them. She was a little out of breath when she got to the top. She and Marcus studied the petroglyphs for a few minutes and then looked out over the view below. "It's beautiful here."

"It is," Marcus agreed, "but it might be more comfortable in the winter."

Sam nodded and started back down the metal stairs.

Everyone mounted their bikes again and made two more brief stops on Campfire Road: *Arch Rock* and the *Fire Cave*. Then they rode the eleven miles to visit *Elephant Rock*, near the east park entrance. Sam was glad that Greg had made an itinerary for them.

The Cardinal, The Fat Boy & The Flamingo

When they arrived at *Elephant Rock*, Cathy joined Sam and Marcus for the short hike. "Well, look at that! It really does look like an elephant!" She laughed, and her eyes twinkled. "Will you take a picture of me, Sam?"

"Of course." She took several and was happy to see Cathy enjoying herself. She didn't notice Marcus move away to talk to Cal, but Cal caught her eye when he started waving his arms around. His voice carried when he shouted at Marcus. "She sent you over here, didn't she?"

Marcus shook his head. Then he said something else and headed toward Greg.

"That was smart, bringing a hat." Cathy regained Sam's attention. "I wasn't thinking about how hot it would be out here." She wiped her hand across the moisture on her forehead.

"Would you like to wear it for a while?"

"Could I? I think that might help. The sun is making me feel tired."

"Did you bring enough water?"

"Yes, I think so."

"I brought a lot, so let me know if you run out."

"Thank you, dear," she said as she placed the large-brimmed hat on her head.

When they returned to the bikes, Lizzy and Dani were waiting there. *Poor things. I hope we find some shade soon, so they can cool off.* Sam pulled a ball cap out of her bag and placed it on her head.

"You changed your hat," Marcus said.

"Cathy needed the sun hat more than I did. Where are we going next?"

"We can see *Seven Sisters* on the side of the road, but Greg wants to get to the Visitor's Center because Lizzy is suffering."

"Okay with me. A little shade will feel good."

They rode back on the Scenic Highway to White Dome Road, then turned right.

Lizzie and Dani practically ran for the shaded pavilion, then plopped on a bench. Pedro took Dani some water.

Dani, not one to suffer in silence, said, "Next time, just leave me at the hotel! I'm gonna have a rash!"

"Sorry," he mumbled.

"You are gonna be sorry!" She took a big gulp of water and then began to cough.

Lizzy patted her back. "Are you okay?"

"Wrong. Pipe." Dani said in between coughs.

Pedro's eyes got huge. "Do you need the Heimlich?"

"No! Idiot! You'd break me!"

Pedro just stared until her coughs started to subside.

Cal wandered over. "There's no cell phone reception here, but I saw a sign that says *Balancing Rock* is only an eighth of a mile. Anyone up for a little walk?"

"I am!" Sam said.

"Me too!" Everyone agreed except Lizzie and Dani.

"I'll stay here," Lizzie said weakly.

"I'll stay here too, I guess." Cathy sat down on the bench beside Lizzie.

Sam looked around and turned to Marcus. "Where'd Rachel go? I haven't seen her for a while."

"She went right up the trail when we got here."

Sam slid her mouth sideways and scrunched her eyebrows. I should check in with her. She's been acting kind of odd, even for her.

"What are you thinking?" Marcus asked.

"I just wonder what she's up to."

They walked to *Balancing Rock*, then stood in awe. Twenty feet in the air, the sandstone formation had eroded in such a way that the top looked like it was balancing precariously. Sam looked at it from every angle and was taking pictures with her phone when she ran into Rachel. "Oh! Hey, Rachel. Is everything okay?"

"Yeah, why?"

The Cardinal, The Fat Boy & The Flamingo

"I just haven't seen you around much today. Do you have enough water?"

"Of course," Rachel said, curling her lip. "Why are you always getting in my business?"

"Sorry." Sam put her hands up. "I was just checking in."

"Well, don't." Rachel stalked back toward the Visitor's Center.

Once they had all returned to the pavilion, Pedro approached the bench where Dani was sitting and said something to her as he held out his hand. They walked toward the restrooms as he continued to talk. They both disappeared for a minute or two before reemerging transformed.

"Oh my god!" Lizzie laughed as Dani approached. She was wearing boxers, a tank top, and a smile.

"Lizzie, you have to do this. Pedro is a genius!"

"I am not walking around in boxers!"

"I thought I was gonna die from heat stroke. This is such a relief! And besides, if we both do it, everyone will just think it's a trend."

Lizzie looked at Greg. "He's much bigger than I am. They would fall right off."

"I have a safety pin," Sam said. "And sunscreen."

"Come on. I'll help you," Dani said. "Greg!" she called. "Can Lizzie borrow your boxers?"

He walked over with eyes as big as saucers. "Brilliant! I'll be right back."

"I'll go get the pin and the sunscreen." Sam walked back to her bike and fished around in her saddlebags.

Once she and Greg returned, Lizzie and Dani disappeared into the restroom.

When they reemerged, the oddly dressed pair were smiling and hamming it up.

"I need a picture of this!" Pedro said. "Sam, will you take one of the four of us?"

Sam took his phone and got several fun shots.

"Since you two missed so much, how about we do the 3.3-mile loop through *Pastel Canyon*, *Fire Wave*, and *White Domes* slot canyon?" Greg asked. "We can see all the best stuff."

Everyone agreed, and they headed back to their bikes.

"I wonder how long they'll be smiling once we're hiking," Marcus whispered.

"At least they've shed their leathers. That must have been terrible."

They pulled off and parked in the gravel near the entrance to *Pastel Canyon*. Sam was glad they decided to do the loop. *Pastel Canyon* was even more beautiful than she had hoped. "It looks like swirls of sherbet," she said.

Marcus nodded. "Amazing colors." He stopped. "Hold on, I forgot my cap."

Sam watched him jog back to his bike, then got distracted by the colors again. She took pictures from every angle, but they didn't do the canyon justice.

Even Dani and Lizzie were oohing and ahhing as they walked the short half mile to the *Fire Wave*.

The polished sandstone gleamed in the late afternoon sun. "Pictures don't really show how breathtaking it is," Sam said sadly. "Let me take one of you in front of the canyon wall. Maybe your black shirt will bring out the colors."

Marcus stood where she pointed and said, "Cheese!"

"Thanks!"

"You should have one too. Let me take one."

Sam threw her arms out and her head back when he took her picture.

"Look. I think your hair did the trick."

They both smiled over the picture and then sped up to rejoin the group.

Coming out of *Pastel Canyon* and onto the *Fire Wave*, everyone gazed in awe. The narrow canyon opened into a wide panorama.

The Cardinal, The Fat Boy & The Flamingo

The red and white striated sandstone became an undulating path underfoot. And the wave curled around and up toward a final viewpoint. Visitors milled around taking pictures.

The *Fire Wave* narrowed toward the top, and Cal walked quickly past people who were waiting until he was standing at the very edge. Rachel was not far behind him. He looked over the edge, threw his arms in the air in victory, then took a drink out of his water bottle. Cal looked at the water bottle before throwing it violently over the edge of the cliff. His eyes bulged, and he grabbed his throat and doubled over. People near him started backing away. Rachel was stuck trying to tie her shoe but tried to scoot away from the edge. Cal wasn't paying attention to his feet and stepped off the cliff, his eyes and mouth wide as he fell.

There was a moment of complete silence as everyone froze in shock. Then, at the sound of Cal's body hitting the rock below, Rachel began to scream. Sam watched everyone leap into action. Lizzie stared dumbfounded and put her arms around Dani. Dani buried her face against Lizzie, her shoulders convulsing. Greg and Pedro rushed towards the edge, along with some other tourists. Sam looked at Marcus, then set off at a run to see if she could help. She heard Cathy asking Rachel if she was okay.

Rachel had stopped screaming and was staring at the place where Cal had stood a moment before. Greg carefully approached the edge and looked down, then he turned with a frown. "We need to get down there and see if he's still alive. Can someone call 911?"

"There's no reception here. I can try from the parking lot," Sam said.

"Ok. Go! Run!" Greg commanded. "Pedro, come with me. Does anyone know a way down?"

Sam ran. Her long strides propelled her down the wave and out of view.

Someone nearby said, "There's a path on this side, but it's a scramble."

"Let's see if we can make it. Can you lead the way?" Greg asked him.

Cathy was trembling as her trauma washed over her. She looked at Rachel and rallied as the men moved away. "Are," she gulped and blinked. "Are you okay?"

Rachel looked up, her face frozen. Her eyes were very round, but she had no other expression on her face.

"She must be in shock," Cathy said to whoever was listening. "Is this yours?" She bent to pick up a discarded Tupperware containing a sandwich.

Rachel grabbed it and flung it over the cliff. "How could anyone eat at a time like this?" She glared at Cathy, then crawled toward the edge and looked down. Cathy moved cautiously forward too and saw a line of men working their way toward the bottom.

"He looks odd from here." She touched Rachel's shoulder and began to back away from the edge. "Let's try to find some shade."

Rachel shrugged Cathy's hand away and stayed where she was.

Cathy felt sick. Seeing Cal fall brought back Roy's murder, and she couldn't help but wonder. *I need Sam. I hope she gets back soon.*

Sam jogged toward the parking lot with her phone held up, trying to find a signal. When she finally had a couple of bars, she dialed Tom. He didn't pick up, so she dialed 911.

"911. What is your emergency?"

"There's been an accident." Sam's voice wavered. "Someone has fallen from the *Fire Wave*. He is either dead or badly injured."

"You're in the Valley of Fire State Park?"

"Yes."

"Please stay on the line."

"Please tell them to hurry."

Sam looked around. Several cars had pulled in, and the parking area was full, but no one had returned from the *Fire Wave*.

Her heart thudded in her chest as she replayed Cal's fall in her mind. *Please, Lord, help him to be okay.*

114

The operator came back on the line as Sam heard approaching sirens. "First responders are on the way."

"Thank you very much. I can hear them."

"Please make yourself visible and direct the responders to the location of the emergency."

Tom pulled up first and jumped out of his car. When Sam saw him, her knees almost buckled. She wanted to fling herself into his arms. *Keep it together, Sam. No one needs you falling apart now.* She took a deep breath and approached him as two more vehicles pulled in.

"Are you the person who called in the emergency?" One of the paramedics asked.

"Yes. The problem is that there's no signal over there, and the trail doesn't go to where he fell," Sam said.

"He's below the top of the *Fire Wave*?" one of the officers asked.

Sam nodded, blinking furiously to keep the tears at bay.

"I know the way. Let's move out."

"Who fell?" Tom asked as they rushed toward the scene of the accident. "Was it one of your group?"

"It was Cal, and I'm not sure what happened." Sam swiped at her eyes.

Tom nodded. "Let's see what kind of shape he's in, then we'll find out."

He left Sam and went to talk to the Officer who was leading the way. Sam saw the officer nod before Tom dropped back next to her.

"I wanted to let him know that it might be part of a homicide investigation."

Sam's breath hitched, and her eyes widened. "How could that be?"

"Do you believe in coincidence?" Tom panted from the exertion.

"I don't know. Sometimes."

"I don't." Tom shook his head. They rounded a bend. "Who are all those people?"

Looking ahead, Sam saw Greg and the other men who had gone down to check on Cal. As they approached, the men stepped back out of the way.

Greg said, "We wanted to help him if we could, but he was already dead when we got here. We didn't touch anything except to feel for a pulse."

"How long did it take you to reach him?" asked the paramedic as he knelt down to ascertain that Cal was deceased.

Greg looked at the others, and they shrugged. "I'm not sure. We came down that way." He pointed at a steep, sandy path. "Maybe ten minutes?"

"They started down when I started toward the parking lot," Sam said.

The paramedic said, "It looks like he suffered from anaphylactic shock, as well as the fall. He landed on his back, and his lips, tongue, and face are very swollen. Did he have any allergies?"

"He probably had a food allergy. He was always very careful about ordering when we ate out," Greg said.

The paramedic looked over the body. "Did anyone see him eat or drink anything?"

"He was drinking out of his water bottle before he fell. He threw it away from him after he drank."

"We'll need to find that water bottle," Tom said. "Greg, maybe you can help the officers locate it. I need to go up and talk to the witnesses."

"We'll get the body to the morgue," the paramedic said. "There won't be a lot of clues lying around down here, and the heat is causing rapid decomposition."

"Good point. How do I get up there?"

"Just go back the way we came and turn right."

Tom nodded and began the trek to the top, Sam trailing behind. When they reached the others, everyone turned and stared; all except Rachel, who was still keeping vigil at the edge.

Tom went to the center of the small crowd. "Everyone. I am Detective Thomas Cork. Did any of you see what happened right before Mr. Lenox went over the edge?"

A few people raised their hands, so Tom asked Sam and Marcus, who had joined them, to wait nearby while he spoke with the witnesses.

Chapter 17

Tom passed a notebook to the woman on his right. "Let's go over the events together. You can each write your name and contact information in the notebook. I've also drawn a simple map of this area. Can you tell me where each of you were when it happened?"

Mary, the woman on Tom's right, pointed to the middle of the wave. "My friend Sarah and I were about here. I stopped to look around when I saw a woman at the top stoop to tie her shoe. The guy who went over the edge said something to her and laughed. Then he picked up his water bottle. I don't know why it was on the ground."

"Ok. Stop there. Is that what everyone else saw?

Everyone nodded.

"Did anyone see him put the bottle down?"

"I was behind the lady who tied her shoe," a man said. "About here." He pointed to the map. "I saw the man put down his water bottle and raise his arms in the air. He shouted, 'Someone should take my picture!' and the lady stopped tying her shoe and looked up at him."

"And your name, sir?"

"Neal."

"Thank you, Neal."

"I was on the other side." A man on Tom's left pointed at the map. "I saw the lady take a water bottle and Tupperware out of her bag as she was walking. I wondered why she was taking them out in that spot. I thought maybe she was looking for her camera." His brow furrowed.

"Then she set everything down and tied her shoe. I'm Ron, by the way."

"Thank you, Ron." Tom glanced at the group. "Did anyone else see that?"

Everyone shook their heads.

"No one?"

Tom asked the two other witnesses where they were and marked them on the map. "Was there anyone else near the top when the accident occurred?"

"There were two men," Ron said. "I think they went down to see if they could help him."

Mary leaned in and said, "One had gray hair and camo shorts, and the other had dark hair and a big mustache."

"I was pretty close, too," Neal added.

"All of you are certain he didn't get pushed."

"No one was close enough to push him," Ron said.

"Is there anything else you noticed? Even something that might seem irrelevant?"

Mary raised her hand. "The man who fell was acting strangely before he fell. I don't know if he was playing around or if something was wrong, but he grabbed his throat."

"Did anyone else notice that?"

Ron nodded. "His eyes got big, and he doubled over."

"Any idea why he did that?"

"He threw his water bottle over the edge. Maybe something tasted bad?"

Tom nodded. "Thank you. Anything else you can think of?"

"After he went over the edge," Neal said slowly, "a chubby lady with curly hair ran to the lady tying her shoe. It seemed like she was trying to console her, but the shoe lady shrugged her off and threw her sandwich. Then she scooted to the edge on her belly like she was afraid of the drop. She stayed there the whole time. She's still there." He pointed at Rachel.

"We didn't want to get too close to her," Mary added.

"Why is that?"

"She didn't seem quite right, and we didn't want to get between her and the edge. Look. She's still there. Would you want to approach her?"

"No. But I imagine I'll have to. Thank you all for your help. Here's my card. Please contact me if you think of anything else."

They each took a card. Neal handed him the notebook before he left.

Tom looked around and saw that the members of *Torque* were all present, and a group of sightseers waited impatiently behind the crime scene tape that had been strung across the entrance. He approached Greg and Pedro. "Did you find the water bottle?"

"Yes. They sent us back here."

"Can you two help me move Rachel away from the ledge? I don't want any more accidents."

They moved toward her, and Tom spoke gently. "Rachel, we're going to have to move away from here. Would you like some help up?"

She glared at him with a dirty, tear-streaked face. "Stay away from me!"

"You will need to come. You can do so of your own volition, or we can help you."

She didn't move, so Tom nodded at Greg and Pedro to each take a side, and together they lifted her off the ground and moved her away from the ledge. She put up a fight, but the three of them were able to move her safely.

"I need to interview all of you, but it might be wise if we get out of the sun. Harvey is bringing some Subway sandwiches. Why don't we meet down at *Seven Sisters*?"

"We all parked by the entrance to *Pastel Canyon*, and Rachel looks like she might need medical attention." Sam raised her eyebrows at Tom.

"I'll have Harvey come here then and phone for another ambulance."

120

Rachel came out of her stupor and started swinging her arms. "I don't need an ambulance! Just leave me alone!" She started stomping toward the parking lot, then stopped and looked around.

"It might be better if Harvey takes her in his cruiser," Tom mumbled to Sam.

"Let me see if we can get any more backup." He stepped away from the group and made his calls.

When Harvey arrived, he ferried the group down to their bikes, then returned for Rachel. He and Tom had to restrain her to get her in the cruiser, but once she was inside, she got quiet. "I'll drive down to *Seven Sisters* and deposit the sandwiches," Harvey said. "Then I'll take her to the nearest hospital."

"Keep me updated," Tom said, mounting his bike.

Sam was sitting at a picnic table in the shade when Tom pulled into the parking lot. She took a big bite of her sandwich and chewed slowly.

"I didn't realize how hungry I was," Marcus mumbled around his food.

"Greg and Pedro must be doubly starved!" Sam said. "Climbing down that steep rock and back up again."

"Yeah. Hungry," Greg said between bites.

Tom walked up, and Sam handed him a sandwich. He looked around. "It's a good thing Harvey brought a lot." Sam smiled at him but kept chewing. They ate in silence until they couldn't eat any more.

After Tom finished his sandwich, he said, "I know you've all had a long, tiring day, but I'd like to get your impressions while they're still fresh in your minds. Let's start with Greg and Pedro since you were closest."

They moved closer to where Tom was sitting.

"I was right behind him," Greg said gravely.

Everyone leaned in to listen.

"What did you notice?"

121

"He got to the top and looked out over the canyon. Then he set his water bottle down and shouted, 'Someone should take my picture.' He bent over and said something to Rachel. It sounded like, 'Come pose with me, baby.' I thought it was weird because everyone knew they hated each other."

"I was a couple steps behind Greg," Pedro said.

"And you saw the same thing Greg did?"

"Mostly. Except Rachel was taking things out of her bag on the way up. Looking for water, maybe? She tripped. Then she stopped and put everything down. I think she was tying her shoe."

"There's no question Cal stepped back and fell? No one could have pushed him?"

They shook their heads.

"No one was close enough," Pedro said.

"Did Cal have any life-threatening allergies?"

"He had allergies, but I don't know if they were life-threatening," Cathy said. "He always asked about ingredients when we ate out."

"He had an EpiPen," Sam added. I saw him put it in his pocket once.

Tom looked at Sam. "Did you notice anything odd at the Fire Wave?"

Sam started to shake her head but then stopped. "Rachel was wearing her gloves."

"Why would she do that? It was so hot," Lizzie said. "Speaking of which, it has cooled off a lot. I'm actually getting chilly."

"She might have been trying not to hurt her hands on the rocks." Sam scrunched up her nose. "But I wouldn't have wanted them on. The reason I noticed is she had to take them off to tie her shoe."

"She didn't have them on when we moved her from the ledge," Greg said. "She scratched me." He showed Tom the red marks on his arm.

"I wonder when she took them off."

Cathy said, "I tried to help her after Cal fell. She was stuffing things back in her bag and didn't have them on."

Tom squinted into the distance, then said, "Okay. I think that's enough for now. Unless anyone has anything to add?"

"I was taking pictures," Marcus said. "Maybe there's something in one of them."

"Let me know. For now, you can all go back to the hotel and get some rest."

There was a group sigh of relief.

"Lizzie and I need to change back into our leathers," Dani said.

"I need to change too," Sam added.

Everyone got up and started moving around, but Tom stopped Sam near her bike.

"Are you alright?"

"Yes. Poor Cal."

"I'll tell you more tomorrow. In the meantime, be careful."

"It wasn't an accident?"

"He was almost certainly helped over the edge."

Chapter 18

Tom rode back with *Torque* toward the nearest hospital and gave them a wave as he made his exit from the highway. Harvey met him at the Emergency Room entrance and asked for the doctor on duty. While they waited, Harvey said, "She was quiet until we pulled up to the hospital entrance. A nurse and an orderly were waiting with a wheelchair. When I opened the car door, Rachel pushed them away and got out of the car on her own. She insisted she didn't need to see a doctor, so I told her it was the hospital or the police station."

"She chose the hospital, I guess."

A petite woman with a large pile of curly red hair strode toward them, her shoes squeaking on the freshly scrubbed tile. She smiled and stuck out her hand. "Hello, I'm Dr. Lacey. How can I help you?"

"I'm Detective Thomas Cork, and this is Detective Brother. We are here about Ms. Simon, who was brought in about two hours ago."

"Do you have a warrant for release of information?"

Harvey handed it to her, and she nodded.

"Ms. Simon is perfectly fine. I asked her to recount what happened this afternoon. Her voice shook, and she cried off and on, but her reactions were normal. She was probably dealing with shock. I gave her a prescription to help her relax if she needs it."

"What did you prescribe?" Tom asked.

"A week's supply of Valium."

"Do you have her belongings?"

"Yes. Except her phone. She didn't want to let go of that."

"May I speak to her?"

"Yes, of course."

"Then could you get her belongings for Detective Brother while he waits?"

Dr. Lacey smiled and nodded. "Here is her room, Detective."

"Thank you for your time, doctor. Here's my card in case you think of anything else."

She took his proffered card and led Harvey back the way they came.

Tom knocked on the door and opened it. "Hello Ms. Simon." He watched her slide the phone under her pillow. "Dr. Lacey has given you the all-clear and said you are able to answer some questions."

Rachel's eyes narrowed, and she shrunk back a little. "Sure."

Tom pulled up a folding chair and sat down. "We've heard what happened from several people, but I would like your version of events."

"Where should I start?" She spread her hands.

"Your group headed up the *Fire Wave*. You and Cal were in front?"

"I was in front, but I slowed because there was a group waiting in front of me."

"Can you describe any of them?" Tom leaned back in the chair and crossed an ankle over his knee, using body language to put her at ease.

Rachel's eyes rolled up as she thought back, but then she shook her head. "It's all a jumble now."

"So, you slowed down. Then what happened?"

"Cal marched right past me and pushed his way to the front. Then he threw his arms in the air and said, *Someone should take my picture*."

"And where were you?"

"I was a few feet from him when I tripped and realized my shoe was untied. I stopped to tie it."

"At what point did Cal put his water bottle down?"

Rachel's eyes widened. "His water bottle? There was no water bottle around where he fell."

Why is she lying? "What did he say to you when he picked up the water bottle?"

"I told you there was no water bottle."

Tom put his foot down and leaned forward. "There was, and we have found it. What did he say to you?"

Rachel leaned backward in response. "He said something like, *Want to join me, babe?* I don't remember. He was just being stupid."

Tom rubbed his chin. "How about your backpack? Were you looking for something?"

Rachel's face was blank.

"Several people said you were taking things out of your backpack on the way up."

She shook her head. "I don't know. I don't remember. I might have been looking for my camera." She shrugged.

"What did Cal do right before he fell?"

"I don't know what he was doing. I was tying my shoe, and he started dancing around."

"You didn't look up to see?" Tom's forehead wrinkled. *She must be the worst witness I have ever seen.*

"Look. I was mad at him, okay?" She crossed her arms. "I was ignoring him because I was mad. I should have been paying attention, and I wasn't. I feel like a really bad person. I feel like I should have done something, but I didn't, and now he's dead." Tears were coursing down Rachel's face. "Maybe it's my fault. I didn't mean for him to die." She hunched, and her shoulders convulsed.

"Ms. Simon. Look at me, please."

She looked into his kind eyes.

"Unless you replaced the contents of that water bottle, you did *not* kill him. There was nothing you could have done. Did you swap either the bottle or the contents?"

"No! I didn't even see a water bottle other than mine."

"What did you have in yours?"

"Water, of course."

"Then you can stop blaming yourself. You may have been angry with him, but anger didn't kill him."

"Rachel sniffed. Thank you, detective."

Harvey entered the room and nodded at Tom.

"I think that will be all, for the moment," Tom said, "except we will need to borrow your phone."

"They took it when I arrived," Rachel said.

"Why don't you go with Detective Brother and ask?" He nudged her toward Harvey. She looked back at him as they left.

Tom waited a second, then got up and took the phone from underneath Rachel's pillow. He walked toward the nurse's station.

Rachel said, "You have it, don't you."

He smiled. "We will return all of your belongings after the analysts have looked through them. Is there any additional information you would like to share with us?"

"No." She shook her head.

"Would you like a ride back to your hotel?"

"Yes, please."

Tom stowed Rachel's belongings in his saddlebags and waved as Harvey and Rachel walked toward the cruiser.

Chapter 19

The next morning Cathy was surprised when Rachel sat down with her at the Cup of Cappuccino. "Hello, dear. Are you feeling better?"

Rachel nodded glumly.

"I had no idea you and Cal had gotten so friendly."

"It was very recent. Could we not talk about it?"

"Of course, dear." Cathy patted her hand. "Would you like me to order you a latte?"

"No. That's okay. I just wanted some company."

Cathy smiled at her. *She sure has changed.*

"When Roy died, did you have all kinds of things in your head that you wished you had asked him or said to him?"

"I wished I had told him I loved him that morning. We had a stupid argument, and I wished I could have told him I was sorry."

Rachel nodded and looked at her hands. "Did you know anything about his business?"

"No, he didn't want me to know for some reason. I had wondered if it was illegal. Did Cal keep things from you too?"

"Yes, he was very secretive," Rachel mumbled. "I've gotta go. Thanks for talking to me, Cathy." She gave a small smile and a wave as she left.

Such a strange young woman. Cathy looked around and saw Sam waiting in line. She waved to get her attention. "Sam! Over here!"

"Good morning, Cathy. You seem chipper today." Sam put her latte and a scone on the table and sat down. "No ill effects from yesterday?"

"Not really. I have a little sunburn, and I've been thirsty.

I am really confused about what's going on, though. It must be one of us since Cal died away from the hotel?"

"Yes, I think so."

"These are my friends, people I've spent years with. I just don't understand." Cathy shook her head and looked into her cup as if it held the answer.

"The police will figure it out."

They sat silently for a moment, then Sam said, "Do you know anything about flamingos? The symbolism?"

Cathy looked at Sam, and her eyebrows rose. "Flamingos?"

"I keep dreaming about them. I know we're at the Flamingo hotel, but usually, my recurring dreams mean something. Marcus said something about perspective."

"That's true. Looking at your situation from a different angle. That's because they eat with their heads upside down. Can you imagine?" Cathy's laugh tinkled sweetly. "I have a flamingo tattoo. Roy thought it was my spirit animal."

"Really? Why?"

"They are supposed to mean someone is flamboyant, fun, and expressive."

Sam grinned. "That does sound like you."

"I know. Right? What are you up to today?"

"I haven't really decided. Maybe I should get a tattoo."

"Your first?"

Sam nodded.

"I have to go with you then! A first tattoo is a rite of passage! What were you thinking of getting? It should have a special meaning."

"There are two options. My cousin said he is nicknamed the Crow in his professional circles, and he dubbed me the Cardinal. My hair matched a special painting by my grandmother. Jack said we are birds of a feather. So, I could either get a tattoo of a cardinal or one of a cardinal and a crow."

"How important is Jack?"

"Very."

"Then do both. He is family, and he'll always be there for you."

Sam's eyes got a little teary, and she nodded.

Cathy stood. "Well?"

"What? Now?"

"No time like the present! I know a place."

"Of course you do," Sam muttered.

"Let's go! I am so excited." She took Sam's hand and pulled her out of the coffee shop.

"The victim went into anaphylactic shock before he hit the ground," Mike reported. "He wore a bracelet warning of his milk allergy. He might not have died if he had been able to get his EpiPen in time or if he hadn't gone over the cliff. I'm not sure which one actually killed him."

"What have you found regarding the thermos?" Stewart asked.

Patricia said, "The water bottle contained whole milk. There were no prints other than one set of the victim's. It looks like it was wiped clean before he picked it up."

Tom frowned. "Rachel, who was nearby and claimed there was no water bottle, had an identical one in her bag. Have you run the prints on that one?"

"Yes. One set of prints."

"Want to take bets they're Cathy's?"

"Why Cathy's?" Harvey asked.

"Because Rachel was wearing gloves, and Cathy helped her pick up her things."

Stewart looked at Herb from IT. "Have you found anything on the phone?"

"She didn't have any texts or contacts on the phone. Her last call was to a burner phone."

"Did anyone try calling that number?" Tom asked.

"Yes. An angry-sounding woman answered and started yelling about Rachel leaving the hospital and not letting her know."

Stewart looked at Tom. "Did the hospital report anyone showing up?"

"Yes. A woman named Marsha Carey. She said she was Rachel's sister. Claire is running a background check as we speak."

"Good." Stewart nodded. "Any thoughts about how the two murders fit together?"

"Cal Lenox was a blackmailer. He may have pressed the wrong person."

"Next steps?"

"Harvey and I will interview the rest of *Torque*. I'll get together with Sam later and see if she's learned anything."

The captain smirked a little. "Sounds good. Keep me informed."

"Do you want to have dinner and observe our suspects again?" Tom asked.

"Sure. We can see if the dynamic has changed. Let me know where and when."

Tom nodded and walked back to the cruiser.

Sam loved her new tattoo. She admired it with Cathy in the mirror. A cardinal and a crow circled each other in an upward spiral.

"It's beautiful!" Cathy said. "I love it."

"Can I take a picture for my portfolio?" the artist asked.

"Sure, but don't give anyone else the exact same one, okay?"

"I won't," he assured her. "I'm really happy with it, though. Some of my best work."

"I can't wait to show Jack." Sam grinned. "It's even better than what I was picturing."

Once they left the tattoo parlor, Cathy suggested lunch.

They walked down narrow streets lined with high-end shops. Sam felt like she was outdoors, but a high ceiling mimicked the sky, and the temperature was comfortable.

"I know a place," Cathy said. "We can have a nice meal and find you something to wear that won't hurt. Once you take that covering off, your clothes will rub."

"I didn't think about that. I didn't think about not going in the pool, either." Sam frowned a little. Her phone buzzed, and she looked at Tom's text. "Would you mind if Detective Cork joined us for lunch?"

"Not at all," Cathy said. "You kind of like him, don't you."

"Yes, but mostly as a friend. Anything else is hard when you're away from home."

Cathy nodded and pointed toward a fountain. "Tell him, *Trevi*."

Sam texted Tom and followed Cathy around the *Fountain of the Gods*.

"It's really pretty at night."

"I bet it is. It's lovely now. Makes me want to go swimming."

"Do you want to eat inside or by the fountain?"

"It might be quieter inside."

"True." Cathy approached the hostess and asked for a table for three.

Tom arrived just as their table was ready.

"Perfect timing," Sam said.

Tom smiled. "This will be a partially working lunch. I hope you don't mind."

"Fine with me," Cathy said. "As long as you don't hog the bread."

Tom put one hand in the air. "I promise."

"Your server will be with you right away." The hostess handed them each a menu and returned to her post.

"What's good?" Sam asked.

Cathy looked at her menu. "The Marguerite pizza and Caesar's salad are delicious."

"Are the portions large enough to share?"

"It depends how much you eat." Cathy's eyes twinkled.

"Why don't we get one salad and two pizzas? How hungry are you, Tom?"

"Maybe we could get an appetizer too?"

They all agreed. The young, vivacious server bounced over to the table with fresh bread and took their order. After she had bustled away, Tom asked, "What have you ladies been up to this morning?"

Cathy and Sam looked at each other and giggled. "Sam got her first tattoo."

Tom's eyebrows rose a little. "What made you decide to do that?"

"A souvenir, I guess." She shrugged.

He studied her quietly and then said, "I have a few questions I want to ask. Do either of you mind answering together, or should we do them privately?"

"I don't have anything to say that Sam can't hear."

Sam nodded. "Together is fine."

"The two of you seem pretty close, considering you just met."

Sam and Cathy looked at each other. "We are, and we aren't. I think we're comfortable together, but we don't usually talk about highly personal things."

Cathy nodded, then reached out and squeezed Sam's hand. "I don't know what it is exactly, but comfortable is a good word. I trust Sam for some reason, and she doesn't push me to talk about things I don't want to."

They paused when the server returned with their food and extra plates. "Enjoy!" She rushed off again.

Tom watched the ladies put food on their plates, then served himself. He paused for a moment and studied Cathy. "I know it's not great lunch conversation, but could you tell me what happened on the *Fire Wave*?"

Her fork stopped halfway to her mouth. Then she took a bite and began to chew. When she was finished chewing, she took a deep breath. "I saw Rachel and Cal heading to the top."

Tom took a bite of pizza and said, "Mmm."

"Really good," Sam agreed.

"Did you see him put his water bottle down?"

"Yes. He put it down and put his arms in the air like he was posing for some imaginary photographer."

"Then what happened?"

"Everything seemed to happen at the same time. Rachel was juggling things and then suddenly put everything down. Cal was dancing around. When he went over the side, I didn't know what to do. My feet felt frozen to the ground." She looked down.

"You didn't see what happened to the water bottle?"

"No." Cathy looked back up and narrowed her brows. "I think I might have accidentally put it in Rachel's backpack. I tried to ask about her sandwich, but she threw it away from her."

"Tell me about that."

"She had a Tupperware container, a water bottle, and her backpack sitting on the ground beside her. She was acting strangely, so I put her things in her backpack. At least, I thought they were her things."

"Were Rachel and Cal good friends?"

"No. They hated each other."

"Why do you think she reacted the way she did?"

Cathy shrugged. "It's traumatic seeing someone die."

"Have you talked to her since then?"

"Yes. This morning."

"What did you talk about?"

"It's funny. I don't really know." Cathy paused and ate some salad.

Tom rubbed his chin. "What did you notice on the *Fire Wave*?" he asked Sam.

"Marcus and I were quite a ways back. The first I noticed something was wrong, Cal was waving his arms around and bending over, then he stepped back into thin air. People were screaming and shouting; some rushed to the edge to look."

"Did you notice anyone in particular?"

"Greg."

"Have either of you ever seen Rachel with a camera?"

Sam and Cathy both shook their heads.

"Did either of you know about Cal's food allergy?"

"When we ate out, he often asked how things were made."

"We knew he had a food allergy, but he didn't talk about it. What was he allergic to?" Cathy asked.

"Milk."

Sam's mouth made an oh. "That's a tough one. It was life-threatening?"

"Yes. One more question. Do either of you have any idea how Cal's murder might be connected to Roy's?"

"We still don't know why Roy was killed, do we?" Sam asked.

Tom shook his head.

Cathy's shoulders slumped at the mention of Roy. "Cal was not always pleasant, but I still can't imagine who would kill my Roy."

"Maybe he knew something he shouldn't have? Cal, I mean," Sam said. "He did say once that someone was a thief. 'Find the thief, find the murderer,' he said. Did someone steal something from Roy?"

Cathy shook her head, and a tear ran down her cheek. "I wish I knew."

"I'm sorry I've ruined lunch. Can I buy you each a cocktail to make up for my poor manners?"

"I'll have a beer." Sam winked at him. "Why don't you try one of these concoctions, Cathy?" Sam handed her the drinks menu. "The pizza and salad are delicious, by the way. Excellent suggestion."

Cathy chose a fruity cocktail, and they finished their lunch without any more talk of murder.

Tom took the check when they were finished. "Lunch is on me. Thank you for allowing me to join you."

"Thank you for lunch, detective." Cathy gave him a small smile.

"It was good to see you," Sam added.

"I'll text you later," he said. Then he turned with a wave and headed for the cashier.

Alice Kanaka

Cathy watched him go. "He seems like a very nice man. It's too bad you live so far apart."

Sam thought it might be lucky because she knew he wasn't the one. "Should we look for that blouse or dress that you were talking about? Not here, though."

"Do you really want to go shopping now? I'm feeling kind of beat."

"Me too. Want to go rest up a bit?"

"Yes. I think that would be best."

They made their way back to the hotel and rode the elevator in silence.

"See you at dinner," Sam said when Cathy got off on the 21st floor.

Cathy gave her a limp wave as the doors closed.

Chapter 20

As Sam approached the door to her room, the hair on the back of her neck stood on end. The door was cracked open. She continued walking down the corridor and called Marcus.

"Just wait in the stairwell. I'll be there in a few minutes," he said.

Sam waited until she heard the ding of the elevator, then she joined Marcus in the hall. "I don't know if they're still in there or not."

"It's better to be cautious. Stay behind me."

"Do you have a weapon?"

He nodded and put up a finger before quietly pushing the door open.

"I was wondering how long I'd have to wait," Rachel said, rising from a chair by the window. When she saw Marcus, she shrieked, "What are you doing here?" Then she saw Sam behind him and deflated back into the chair.

"Why are you in my room? And why is my safe open?"

"Don't worry. I didn't take your baby gun. I am looking for something specific."

"Well, whatever it is, I don't have it."

Rachel looked around with disdain. "You don't have much of anything."

"Just the necessities. Would you leave now?"

"Need some alone time with your girlfriend?" Rachel sneered at Marcus.

Sam stared at her for a moment, then walked to the phone and called the front desk.

"What are you doing? We need to talk."

"Hello. An uninvited guest somehow let herself in my room while I was gone, and she won't leave."

Rachel crossed the room and hung up the phone.

"They'll have the room number."

"I'll be quick. Cal told me someone stole something valuable from Roy, and I want to know what it is."

"How would I know that?"

"You might not, but he would." Rachel pointed at Marcus.

He tilted his head. "I don't know of anything that's been stolen, but even if I did, why would I tell you?"

"Roy made me some promises, and I intend to make sure he keeps them." She put her hands on her hips. Her long, acne-scarred face shone with malevolence. "You have until tomorrow to get me that information."

"Or what?"

"You'll see. And you won't like it."

She stomped to the door and ran into a large security guard. He stopped her with his hand. "Is this the intruder?"

"Yes. I'd like to know how she got in."

He looked down at Rachel and tilted his head. "Well?"

"It was open. I just walked in to wait."

"It was not open. I remember closing it this morning."

"Check with the maid then. It was open." She pushed the guard's hand away and strode down the hall.

"Not much I can do in this situation, ma'am." He seemed apologetic, but Sam could see his point.

"You could file a police report and ask them to look at video footage of the hallway."

"No, but thank you anyway. I don't think it's worth pursuing right now."

The guard nodded and walked down the hall.

"Thank you for coming, Marcus. I was really freaked out when I saw the door was open."

"I would have been too. Will you be okay now?"

"Yes. I'll see you at dinner."

Once Marcus had gone, Sam sat down on her bed and removed her shoes. She picked up her phone to call Jack, then she put it back down. *I want to go home. I miss the land and the quiet. I miss Ghost.* Sam thought of riding her fog-colored horse and the cats. *I hope she doesn't think I abandoned her. At least Chiquito and Preciosa have each other. I wonder if Jack has visited them.* She picked up her phone again and dialed.

"Jack Olivares," he answered.

"Hi, Jack."

"Sam! I've missed you. Are you back home?"

"No. I can't leave yet."

"I did get a call from a detective in Las Vegas. What happened?"

Sam told him about Torque and the murders.

"Do you need me there? Are you in danger?"

"I don't think so. I just wanted to hear your voice."

Jack paused. "You know I love you, and we'll always be family." He paused again. "But I can't move to Santo Milagro. My career is too important to me."

"I understand, Jack. I would feel the same way about giving up the ranch."

They were both silent.

"Will you come up for holidays and weekends when you're free?"

"Absolutely! Tell me when you get back, and we'll plan something."

"Okay. You're welcome any time." Sam blinked away moisture from her eyes.

"Talk to you soon."

"Yep. Soon."

They hung up, and Sam just sat for a while. She knew deep down that Jack wouldn't move to Santo Milagro, but it was still a blow hearing him say it.

She also knew that her discontentment at home wasn't his fault. *It's me. I need to find something that inspires me.*

Sam stayed in her room the rest of the afternoon. She read for a while, enjoying the quiet solitude. Skipping dinner had crossed her mind, but she was concerned about missing something that might be useful to Tom.

At a quarter to seven, Sam walked to *Park on Fremont*. It was Lizzie's choice, and Sam was completely unprepared. The front of the restaurant seemed to blend in with its neon surroundings, but as she walked through the interior, the ambiance changed to warm wood and chandeliers. Continuing through to the secret garden in the back, Sam was enchanted by the plants, fairy lights, and colorful, patio-style furniture.

Lizzie approached her from a group of tables set off to the side. "You found us. Isn't it lovely?"

"It's so beautiful. I love it!"

"I get tired of the hectic pace of the city. This garden is like a little oasis." Sam felt drawn to this gentle, genuine version of Lizzie.

Lizzie's shoulders tensed as they walked toward the rest of the members of Torque.

"Is everything okay?"

"Yes, of course." She turned her back on Sam and said brightly, "Look who I found."

"Am I the last to arrive?"

"No, Rachel's not here yet," Marcus said. "Come, sit here with me."

"You just want to steal my food."

"Maybe." He grinned.

They were busy placing their orders when Tom and Stewart surreptitiously took their seats. Sam wanted to turn around because she could sense Tom's presence, but she didn't want to blow his cover. Instead, she concentrated on her food and the conversation around her.

"Everyone seems to be in good spirits," she whispered to Marcus.

"Interesting, isn't it?"

Sam nodded. *I wonder if it's because two people are missing or if someone is happy about something?*

Dani, watching, as usual, said, "Do you two lovebirds have any announcements for us?"

"Not at the moment." Marcus winked at her, and she blushed.

Pedro saw the interaction and started to bluster when Cathy stood. She wobbled and held onto the table. "Lizzie, could you help me to the ladies' room? I seem to have had a little too much to drink."

Lizzie took Cathy's elbow and steered her in the right direction.

Greg watched them leave with an inscrutable expression. He leaned over toward Pedro and said, "If anything happens to me, you'll take care of Lizzie, won't you? I don't want her to end up alone."

"Of course, man. We're family." Pedro patted Greg on the arm.

Dani narrowed her eyes.

The festive atmosphere Sam felt somehow faded away as dinner came to a close. Lizzie and Cathy didn't return. When the others left, Sam leaned toward Marcus again and said, "I want to stay for a while. You don't have to stay if you don't want to."

"I'll stay. This place is nice."

"I wonder what happened to Rachel."

"Who knows. Maybe she found a man."

"Wasn't she with Cal?"

Marcus gaped at her. "She hated him! There is no way!"

"Maybe she acted like she hated him because he rejected her."

"No. It was something else."

Sam thought about that. "She's a puzzle."

The waiter came by, and Sam ordered another margarita. Marcus ordered a whiskey sour.

"I wonder how Cathy got drunk so fast. Did she start drinking before dinner?"

"I don't know. I got here right before you did. But she's not usually a lightweight."

The waiter came back with their drinks, and Sam asked him about Cathy.

"She didn't seem to be drinking more than anyone else."

"Thanks. I was just wondering."

The waiter wasn't listening, though. He was staring at Marcus, who had his arm slung over the back of Sam's chair. "You're with Darren, right?"

"Yeah." Marcus smiled.

"Why are you here with her," he blurted.

"This is my friend, Sam. Were you wanting to ask her out?"

The waiter wrinkled his nose.

"That's not very nice!" Sam said.

"He's young. He'll learn some manners when he's older."

The young man turned and fled back to the kitchen.

"Does Darren have a lot of groupies?"

"You might say that." Marcus smiled.

"Are you planning to stay here when Torque leaves?"

"I don't know. I like Darren, but I don't like the lifestyle. I have to think about it some more. How about you?"

"I'll head home. I've been away long enough."

Sam forgot Tom was in the restaurant, so she was startled when he laid his hand on her shoulder. "Greg has just reported a theft. He said the stolen property belonged to the two of you," he said, looking at Marcus.

Marcus seemed to shrink before Sam's eyes as he groaned in pain. "Are you heading over there?"

"Yes. Why don't you come with us?"

"Did he say what happened?" Sam asked.

"He said his safe was open and empty. He found a piece of paper lying inside. It said It said 'thief'."

Sam's mind went back to finding Rachel in her room with the safe open. Looking at Marcus' compressed lips, she thought he probably remembered too. She realized there was quite a bit they hadn't told Tom. "Tom, can we stop by the front desk and ask for a master key?"

Chapter 21

After Tom had secured a key card, Sam said, "Marcus, you head on up to Greg's room and see what's going on, okay? We have to make a short detour."

She and Tom got off the elevator on the 21st floor. "I have some things to tell you, but I want to go to Rachel's room first. She might need medical attention."

They walked down the hall, and Tom knocked. He knocked again, then used the key card to enter. Flipping on the lights, they found Rachel lying on her bed, next to an empty pill bottle. Tom grabbed the bottle and read the label before calling for an ambulance and the hotel doctor.

"I'll be right back." Sam jogged down the hall to Cathy's room and banged on the door.

Lizzie opened the door with tired eyes. "Sam!" She took a step back.

"Hi, Lizzie. How's Cathy doing?"

"She seems okay. Just sleeping."

Sam narrowed her eyes. "What did you slip into her drink?"

"What? Nothing!" Lizzie put her hand on her chest. "Why would I put something in her drink?"

"Someone did. You were sitting next to her."

"So was…" She stopped.

"Who else was sitting next to her?" Sam tilted her head.

"I don't remember."

Sam nodded. "I remember, though."

"Why would Greg do something like that?"

"I have no idea. Stay with her, please. I'll send a doctor."

The Cardinal, The Fat Boy & The Flamingo

Sam got back to Rachel's room as the paramedics were taking her out on a gurney. "Someone should check on Cathy too," she told Tom.

He spoke to the doctor, then waved Sam over and had her sit down at the small table by the window. "Explain to me what I'm missing."

"Remember when we went to Omnia, and I was going to tell you something?"

Tom crossed his arms and tapped his foot a couple of times.

"Roy invited Marcus to join Torque and help with the family business."

"Which was?"

"Buying and selling rare coins. Marcus invested everything he had, then Roy died, and the coins went missing."

Tom rubbed his chin.

"Marcus thought Greg might have them, so he talked me into helping him break into the Scotts' room. I wanted to tell you, but I didn't want to put you in a difficult position."

Sam saw the look on Tom's face and was suddenly worried that she might have ruined their friendship. His eyes looked like storm clouds, and his fists were clenched.

"Tell me what happened."

"We waited for Greg to leave, then Marcus used a key card to get in. I don't know where he got it."

Tom just looked at her.

"I stood just inside the door while Marcus looked for the coins. He said he wanted me there so I could be a witness that he didn't take anything that didn't belong to him."

"Did he find them?"

"Greg came back early and was bellowing and waving his gun around. When we explained why we were there, he calmed down and admitted that Roy gave them to him for safe keeping."

Tom put his and to his chest.

"I left them discussing next steps."

Tom paced.

"Before you start yelling, there's something else."

"You are going to give me a coronary."

Sam held up her hand. "When I got back to my room this afternoon, the door was ajar, and I was afraid to go in. I called Marcus, and he met me in the hall.

When we went in, the safe was open, and Rachel was sitting at the table."

Tom closed his eyes briefly. "What did she want?"

"Rachel always speaks in riddles. She said something about Roy owing her, and she was looking for something specific."

"The coins?"

"Probably, but I don't think she knew what she was looking for."

He blew air out of his nose. "So, what are you getting at?"

"The safes in this hotel don't seem secure. Roy's was open at his murder scene. Marcus opened Greg's, and Rachel opened mine."

"So at least two or three people know how to open them."

"Right. Also, Rachel was not at dinner, so she looked like a good suspect. I believe someone also put something in Cathy's drink. She was acting very drunk halfway through dinner, and Lizzie helped her to her room." Sam sat and waited for Tom to see her point.

"You think Rachel was meant to be the scapegoat, and Lizzie was taken out of the picture?"

"That's what it looks like to me."

Tom paced. "So, Greg stole the coins himself?"

"None of them were ever his, to begin with."

"Where would he have put them?" He frowned.

"I don't know. I've never even seen them. In fact, the only people who claim to have seen them are Greg and Marcus." Sam's mouth formed an o. "Maybe they never had them and are trying to find them."

Tom held up his hands. "So, if they exist and Greg actually had them, maybe he left them at the front desk or in the hotel safe."

"We can ask."

"Does this tie into the two murders?"

Sam tilted her head. "Don't you think so?"

"Yes, I do. Why didn't you let Marcus join us?"

"I really like Marcus, but if they don't actually have the coins..." Sam shook her head sadly. "I really hope I'm wrong. Let's go see what's happening upstairs."

Sam felt a sense of deja-vu when the elevator opened, and they were greeted by the sight of uniforms. Before they entered the Scotts' room, Sam stopped and put her hand on Tom's arm. When his eyes met hers, she said, "I am really sorry. I should have told you. Can you forgive me?"

"I need a little time to process, but it'll be okay."

"I understand." She followed Tom into the Scotts' room and looked around.

Tom approached Stewart and Harvey for a brief update. Marcus and Greg were standing in a corner with crossed arms and down-turned mouths. Sam joined them. "Any updates yet?"

"No. They're checking for fingerprints," Marcus said glumly.

"Who could have done this?"

"Rachel, of course. She broke into your safe. She wasn't at dinner."

"Would she know how to sell them? Maybe we could follow her on the day of the coin fair."

"She wouldn't be that stupid," Greg mumbled.

"It's worth a shot, isn't it?"

"What would I do without you?" Marcus gave Sam a side hug. "You are always so full of ideas."

Sam smiled at him. *Please don't let him be a bad person.*

A police officer approached and addressed Greg and Marcus. "I have a couple more questions, just to clarify." He led them away, so Sam sat on the sofa to wait.

Marcus returned with slumped shoulders. "Thanks for waiting, Sam. They don't seem to think they'll be able to find the coins.

I have no idea what I'm going to do. I need to talk to Darren."

"Where's Lizzie?" Greg asked glumly

"I'll go get her," Sam said. "I can stay with Cathy if she's still unwell."

"Thanks," Greg said gruffly. He poured himself a drink and sat on the sofa as she let herself out.

Tom and Stewart were still in the hall.

"Did Rachel's room look disturbed at all?"

They both looked at her.

"Assuming someone forced her to take the Valium and that they might have been looking for something?"

"Her room was unusually neat," Stewart said.

Sam stared off into space, thinking. "Well, I am going to visit Cathy and give Lizzie a break."

"Let's compare notes tomorrow morning. I'll buy you a latte," Tom said.

"Anything for a latte. Nine o'clock?"

Tom agreed, and she strode down the hall toward the elevator bank.

Sam had to knock a couple times because Lizzie had fallen asleep. "Greg's asking for you, so I told him I'd give you a breather. Why don't you go get some rest?" Sam smiled.

"Thank you, Sam. The doctor came and took a look at her. He said she'll be fine once she wakes."

"That's very good news."

"I'll check back in the morning." Lizzie left, and Sam got comfortable in the recliner. She dozed off several times before Cathy woke. She was mostly speaking gibberish, but Sam responded as well as she could.

Cathy gradually started making more sense. "What happened? Did I drink too much?"

"I think someone put something in your drink. Do you have any idea who might have done that? Or why?"

Cathy's mouth made a round oh. "Maybe they found out. I'm afraid."

"Found out what?"

"He told me not to tell anyone."

"Anyone in *Torque*? Maybe you could tell the police."

"Yes, maybe." She slept again.

Sam was confused. She used the quiet time to think. *Everyone seems to be looking for a treasure of sorts. Was that why Roy was killed? Who murdered Cal? Did he see something he shouldn't have?*

Sam dozed again and woke to Cathy packing her bags. Alarmed, she said, "What are you doing?"

"I'm leaving. I feel so unsafe."

"Where will you go? Will the police let you leave? You can come stay at my ranch if you like."

Cathy stopped what she was doing. "You are such a dear. Roy left me well-taken care of, but someone killed him. Last night one of my supposed friends put a pill in my drink. Someone is looking for something and doesn't mess around when people are in the way. What happened while I was sleeping?"

"Greg reported a theft. Lizzie stayed with you until I came. Rachel took or was given an overdose of Valium."

"What was stolen?"

Sam looked away for a moment, then decided that honesty was the best policy. "Some coins that Roy and Marcus invested in."

Cathy pursed her lips, and her eyebrows narrowed. "Have you seen these coins?"

Sam shook her head.

"Can you ask your detective friend to come talk to me?"

It was early, but Tom agreed to speak with Cathy as soon as he could get to the hotel. Cathy finished her packing, then sat on the edge of her bed and pulled out her knitting. Sam alternately sat on the edge of her chair and paced.

"You need to find a hobby for times like this." Cathy gave her a weak smile.

"Perhaps I do. I don't know if I'd have the patience for knitting, though. What are you making?"

"I'm not sure yet." Cathy chuckled. "I guess I had better decide before I get too far along."

There was a knock on the door, and Sam went to answer it.

"Good morning." Tom smiled at her. "I have to admit, I'm curious."

Sam let him in, relieved that he seemed to have recovered from her admission the night before. "Would you like me to leave while you talk?" she asked Cathy.

"No. You can stay. I trust you."

Tom put his hands in his pockets. "So, what's this about?"

Cathy took a deep breath and let it out with a little shudder. "I'm afraid. Sam caught me packing my bags this morning. I was going to run away."

"Why are you afraid?"

"It's a long story, really." She put her knitting aside. "Roy and I always told each other everything, but we pretended like we didn't. One reason for that is because of Greg. Greg threw Roy under the bus in the service and never would admit it."

"So, Roy didn't really trust him," Tom said.

"Right." She looked down at her hands and picked at her cuticles, then looked back at Tom. "The only certainty is that he loves Lizzie. He would do anything to keep her safe and happy."

Tom sat on one of the chairs near Cathy.

"Then Marcus showed up and claimed he was Roy's nephew. Roy wasn't sure if he was. He might be, but he was very interested in the *family* business."

"Roy didn't invite him to join?" Sam asked.

"No." Cathy shook her head vehemently. "Anyway, when we arrived in Vegas, Roy asked me to put his bag of coins in the main hotel safe. They are still there as far as I know."

The Cardinal, The Fat Boy & The Flamingo

Sam stared at her. "Greg said that Roy had given them to him for safe keeping because he was going to divorce you, and he thought you might take them from the safe."

Cathy shook her head slowly. "That's almost comical. I'm afraid I did say 'divorce' rather loudly the morning he died. Lizzie probably overheard me."

"What was that conversation about?" Tom asked.

"Rachel kept throwing herself at Roy, to the point where it started to annoy me. He told her to back off, and she said... how did he put it? She said something like, *Why don't you divorce that old cow? We could have such a great time together.* He told me that, and I screeched, *Divorce?* Then we both laughed and made out a little."

"How did you end up arguing?" Sam asked.

"Oh! We didn't. That was another little game we played. I loved him so much." Cathy's eyes got teary, and her voice wavered.

"Why are you suddenly afraid?" Tom focused on her face.

"Because one of my friends killed my husband, and they drugged my drink last night. At some point, they are going to realize that I have the coins." She had pulled out a linen handkerchief and played with it until it was unrecognizable.

"Where's his gun?"

"I don't know. He always had it on him, so he must have trusted whoever shot him."

Tom rubbed his chin again.

"Did Greg and Roy play golf together?"

"No, I don't think either of them played."

Tom paced. "There are a couple of things we can do while we wrap this up. We can post a police officer outside your room. That might tip our hand, though. Or we could pretend we are arresting you, but then someone might decide to search your room." He looked at Sam. "Do you have any ideas?"

"We could say she took a turn for the worse and admit her to the hospital."

Cathy said, "Is the hospital safe?"

"It could be. A police officer could pose as a nurse or an orderly. And we could have another officer stay in your hotel room in case someone decides to break in."

The three of them looked at each other and nodded.

"Let me call an ambulance then, and we'll whisk you away."

Tom made arrangements, and Sam wanted to ride with Cathy, but he stopped her.

"I can take you over later, but I want to pick your brain first. Let's go have that coffee."

They sat in silence on the patio of *Cup of Cappuccino*. Tom sighed and settled down in his chair. "I feel like I keep going in circles," he said finally. "This last incident was supposed to point at Rachel but ended up pointing straight at Greg."

"Sometimes the simplest solution is the correct one... but we still have some unanswered questions."

"Let's go over those, then."

"There's Marcus. Is he Roy's nephew? Did he invest in the coins? Did Greg trick him?"

"Does Lizzie know anything?"

"Where does Rachel fit in?"

Tom nodded. "Is she just being nosy on her own, or is she working with someone?"

"Are Pedro and Dani innocent bystanders?"

"Pedro and Greg are great friends, right?"

"Right," Sam said, "and there is one more very important question."

Tom looked at her and smiled. "Do we believe Cathy?"

"We should check with the manager."

Chapter 22

Sam was starting to feel the effects of her lack of sleep. She looked up from the swirls of milk in her cappuccino and saw Harvey standing at the entrance, scanning the tables. She waved for him to join them and caught Tom's little smile. He was leaning back in his chair, watching her.

Harvey walked over and sat down.

"What did you find out?" Tom asked.

"Cathy put a bag in the hotel safe when they arrived. The bag contains the coins with documentation and certificates."

"So that corroborates Cathy's story, not only about the coins but also about her relationship with Roy," Sam said.

"The robbery never actually happened." Tom paused. "Why? Why go to all that trouble for something that doesn't even belong to him?"

"If he reported the theft of coins that partially belong to Marcus and then someone else has the coins, he could accuse that person of stealing them," Sam suggested.

"Someone is pointing hard at Rachel. You said Marcus was with you when you found Rachel in your room," Tom said.

"Yes."

"And she wasn't sure what she was looking for."

"That was my impression." Sam took a sip of her cappuccino.

"If Marcus told Greg about that, Greg might have wanted Rachel out of the picture."

"We need to find out who Marcus is and if he's working with Greg," Sam said.

Tom looked at her with soft eyes and a wrinkled forehead.

"I understand how you feel about Marcus, but I don't really think that's our priority. We have two murders to solve, and we're not even sure the coin caper is related."

"Probably is," Harvey mumbled.

"What's that, Harve?"

"You always say you don't believe in coincidences."

"Let's go back to the station and assemble the team. We'll start at the beginning and see if we missed something."

"I'll poke around here," Sam said. "Has anyone checked on Rachel?"

"You can visit Cathy and Rachel. Be careful with Marcus. I'll stop by this evening."

Sam nodded, but she wasn't really listening. Her mind was whirling. *I'll go visit Cathy and Rachel. They might know more.*

Tom and Harvey went back to the station. Tom called ahead, so everyone was waiting. Stewart had his hands on his hips and a determined frown on his face. "What's this about, Tom?"

"I'd like to go back over all of the evidence and see if we missed anything. We can add in new information as we go."

"What do we have for the first murder?" Stewart asked the crime scene analysts.

Patricia looked at her notes. "We have bullets from a 9mm gun, a darkened and very cold room, a smashed watch face, and a small pile of soil. The safe was standing open, and nothing appeared to have been taken."

"Don't forget the two empty wine glasses," Claire added.

"Any prints?"

"No, sir."

"I saw the soil and wondered where it came from. Do you have a photograph?" Tom asked. He examined the one passed to him. "Does anyone know how it ended up as part of the crime scene?"

"There was a potted plant on the balcony, but it didn't seem to have any connection to the crime.

Perhaps the victim was interrupted while he was gardening?"

Tom held out his hand for another photo. "I'd like to get back inside the suite for a look at that pot. None of the alibis are airtight, except for Sam's and possibly Cathy's. Almost all of them lied to me about something."

Stewart nodded.

"How about the second murder?"

"Apparently, Roy gave everyone in the group a green, insulated, Torque water bottle," Harvey said. "I have been trying to find out who could have exchanged Cal's with their own."

"That will be very helpful. We can find out who was away from the group and near either Cal or his motorcycle before or during that last hike. Do you want to pursue that line of inquiry on your own?"

"Yes, sir."

"Someone should also be missing their own water bottle. Do we have anything else on the second murder?"

Patricia raised her hand. "We looked through the victim's phone and found some potentially damaging pictures. I've blown them up so you can see them clearly." She stuck a flash drive into the closest computer and pulled up the first photograph on the monitor.

Tom looked at it carefully. He knew Cal was a blackmailer, but he was still surprised. Pedro was standing in the pool with Rachel, looking down at his hands resting on the triangles of her bikini top. "Next," he said.

The second photo was of Lizzie and a man who reminded Tom of high-level personal security. He held Lizzie's upper arm and had a hard look in his eyes and a deep frown. Lizzie had wide eyes and looked like she was trying to pull away from his grasp. "Who is that man?"

"His name is Anton. He works for Lizzie's father," Claire said.

"That's probably how Cal found out her real identity," Tom mused. "A little too smart for his own good. Next."

The third photo was of Marcus entering the bar on the day of Roy's murder.

The time stamp put it during the time he said he didn't leave. "This is interesting."

"Why?" asked the captain.

"It breaks Marcus' alibi, but Cal wouldn't have known that when he took the picture. I wonder why he took it. Next."

The fourth picture was of Dani entering the plastic surgery clinic. Tom already knew she had gone there. "Are there more?"

"There are hundreds, people and places, but those four seemed the most harmful."

Tom stood. "Harvey, continue with your inquiry but let's tackle Lizzie, Greg, and Marcus together. I'll need a warrant for that room. Then, Harvey and I will interview the subjects in the photos."

"Sounds good," Stewart said. "Keep me updated."

Sam shouldn't have been surprised by the size of the hospital, but she was. Cathy and Rachel were in two different locations, so she focused on finding Rachel first.

The receptionist in the emergency department called for a nurse and told Sam to have a seat. Five minutes later, she heard her name. "Samantha Olivares."

Sam stood and raised her hand. "Here." The crush of people and cacophony made it difficult to determine the nurse's location.

"Ah. There you are. Come with me, please." She swiped her badge, and the double doors opened to the inner sanctum. After a short walk through a maze of corridors, the nurse stopped and said, "Here we are." She knocked and stuck her head in. "Your visitor is here, Ms. Simon."

Sam walked in and was greeted with a smile. "Sam! I'm surprised you came to visit."

"I brought you some goodies too. How are you feeling?"

"Goodies first." Rachel laughed and held out her hand.

"I'm not sure if you have any restrictions. I hope these are ok." Sam handed her a bag and a cup.

Rachel took the bag and stuck her nose in it.

"You are officially my new best friend. Thank you so much. Should I share?"

"No. I already had mine." Sam smiled.

Rachel pulled out a large blueberry muffin. "I feel like I'm cheating because they're going to release me soon."

"I'm glad you're feeling better. I heard you almost died." Sam looked around for a chair.

"It would have been worse, but I threw some of the pills up, and they pumped my stomach. They said I'm lucky you found me when you did." Rachel broke off a piece of the muffin and stuck it in her mouth.

Sam tilted her head. "Do you know who gave you the Valium?"

Rachel finished chewing. "It must have been Greg. He came to my room to have a drink with me. They told me that my entire bottle of Valium was gone. Why would he do that?"

"I don't know. Cathy also had one stuck in her drink at dinner. At least, I'm assuming it was a Valium. I don't actually know." She carried a folding chair to the side of the bed and sat down.

Rachel took a sip of coffee. "What else happened last night?"

"Greg reported a theft from the safe in his room."

"What did he say was stolen?"

"Collectors' coins."

"So that's the missing treasure." Rachel narrowed her eyes.

"You thought Marcus had them?"

"Oh, yeah. Sorry about breaking into your room. I still think Marcus has them, or he knows where they are." She took another bite of muffin.

Sam didn't think so. "How well do you know him?"

"Not well at all. We were hanging out together when we were both new. But then he found out about me and Roy."

"Why would that bother him?"

"I think he was worried that my loyalty was elsewhere."

Sam watched Rachel tear off another piece of muffin and wondered why Marcus would need her loyalty.

"You said Roy made you promises?""

"At first, he told me he'd always take care of me. He said that his most recent haul would set us up for life."

"And then when you talked about the future, he...?"

"He said I must be insane, that he'd never leave Cathy."

Sam was guessing when she said, "You went to see him the morning he died. Did you kill him?"

"No! I was angry, but I loved him."

"Did Cal see you leaving Roy's room?"

"Yes. He tried to blackmail me. I was so angry at him too, and then I saw his face when he fell. It was terrible." Tears trickled down Rachel's face. "Two people made me mad, and they both died. I started thinking... was it my fault? I didn't wish them dead. Why did they die?" Rachel looked down, and her shoulders shook.

Sam was alarmed. "Rachel, it wasn't your fault. Someone else was angry too. And that someone has been working hard to point a finger at you. Do you have any idea who it might be?"

Rachel looked at Sam with a tear-streaked face. "They could be provoking." She sat and thought for a moment. "At first, I thought it was Cathy or Marcus. But I know it was Greg who gave me the Valium."

"I can see why you might think it was Cathy, but why Marcus?"

"Roy suspected Marcus wasn't who he said he was, and Cal had dirt on everyone."

"Has Marcus ever told you anything about his family?"

"No, Roy asked me to try to get close to him, but he wasn't interested."

"And what do you think about Greg now?"

"I don't know. I thought he and Roy were best friends." Rachel shook her head. "Poor Roy."

"Did you actually love him?"

"I thought so, but not really. I was in love with the idea of a kind, mature man taking care of me."

"What about Cathy?"

Rachel shrugged. "She always seemed so independent and confident. I didn't think she cared much about him."

Sam smiled sadly. "You seem independent and confident too."

"Cathy's aged ten years since he died. I think their relationship kept her young. I never would have interfered if I had known."

Sam nodded but stayed silent. Someone in Torque has wreaked a lot of havoc. "Do you need a ride back when they release you?"

"I can call an Uber."

"Let me know if you need a ride or some company. I have another visit to make, but I don't really have any other plans."

"Thanks, Sam. I appreciate the goodies and the chance to talk."

They hugged briefly, and Sam left to see Cathy.

Cathy was tucked away on the other side of the hospital in post-surgical care. Sam found her playing cards with the chaplain. She was wearing a hospital gown over shorts and a t-shirt.

"Hello dear," she said when she saw Sam. "Would you like to play?"

"No, thank you. I just stopped by to see how you're doing. I brought some goodies."

Cathy clapped like a child. "Ohh, what did you bring?"

"I brought In 'N Out, but I'm afraid it's cold now."

"No worries. We have a microwave," the chaplain assured her. "Why don't we take a break? I'll heat this up, and you two can chat."

"Thank you, Ruth."

Sam noticed Cathy's eyes had regained some of their sparkle.

"I'm glad you came. I've been thinking."

Sam waited.

"If Greg claimed someone robbed him of something he didn't have, he must not know where it is."

"Yes, that seems logical."

"And he must think I don't know about it."

"Why do you say that?"

"Because if I knew about it, I would either know where it was or know it was missing."

"If he thought you knew where it was, you might be in danger."

"True. He hasn't asked me about it."

"Do you think he could have killed Roy?"

"I don't know."

"What do you know about Marcus?"

"He told Roy he was his nephew. Roy did have a nephew, but both of his parents are dead, so it's hard to confirm."

"Marcus has been telling everyone that he invested his life savings in the coins and that he and Roy were going to sell them at the coin show."

"That can't be true. We kept meticulous documentation. No extra cash or coins came in."

"Something very odd is going on. What do you think about Rachel?"

Cathy thought for a moment. "I think she and I could have been friends if she hadn't tried to steal my husband. She didn't seem to dislike me." Cathy tilted her head and pursed her lips.

"Do you think she could have killed him?"

"No, but then again, I don't know how deep her feelings ran. I got the feeling it was just a game to her."

"Could she have been working with someone else? Trying to run some kind of con, maybe?"

Cathy shook her head. "I just don't know."

The chaplain came back with Cathy's food. "Sorry it took so long. There was a line." She laughed good-naturedly.

"I'll take off now. I'm glad you've found someone to keep you company." Sam smiled and hugged Cathy. "Hopefully, this will be wrapped up soon."

"I sure hope so too! Thanks again for the burger."

Chapter 23

Tom returned to Roy's room with Claire and a warrant. He went straight to the patio, where a pot and a small spade sat in the corner. The plant was dead. They put on gloves, and Tom said, "Let's bag the spade." He felt around in the dry soil until he found what he was looking for. Pulling out a 9mm revolver, he examined it and gave it to Claire. "We might as well take the pot too. It might have prints." Tom stood mumbling to himself about the air conditioner while she finished bagging the evidence. "Will that be all, sir?"

"Yes. Thank you. Call me if you get a match on the gun or any prints." They left the room, and Tom stopped to call Harvey. "Where are you?"

"I'm in the bar. Marcus and the Scotts are here. It seems this is their regular hangout."

"On my way."

When Tom arrived, Marcus was seated with Harvey.

"Good afternoon, detective." He smiled.

"Good afternoon. Did Detective Brother ask you about…"

"Our movements on the day Cal died? Yes."

"So far, from what I've been told, it seems Cal had his water bottle at the Visitor's Center, but then there was a lot of commotion," Harvey said.

Marcus nodded. "Pedro came up with the idea of giving Dani his boxers to wear, then she talked Lizzie into wearing Greg's. Sam went to get a safety pin from her saddlebags. I don't know what else happened, but everyone was moving around."

Tom rubbed his chin. "So, Cal probably put his bottle back in his bag, preparing to go. It got swapped either during the commotion or after you parked at *Pastel Canyon*. Did anything happen after you parked?"

Marcus' eyes went up and to the side, and he pressed his finger against his lips. "I can't really remember. I had to go back for my cap. That sun was hot. But everyone had gone ahead. Sam waited for me."

"One more question. We found pictures on Cal's phone. One was of you, entering the bar when you said you hadn't left."

"I hadn't left. I just hadn't arrived yet."

"Did he try to blackmail you?"

"He showed me the picture, but I just shrugged it off, so he left me alone."

"So, where were you before you came here?"

"Nowhere, really. I was just wandering around."

"Could you give me an example?"

"I don't remember exactly. Most mornings, I get coffee, then I walk along the strip, look at the fountains or the flamingos, people watch, then I come here and hang out with Darren until after lunch. I'm a creature of habit."

"Did Greg show you the coins when you and Sam went to his suite?"

"She told you about that?" Marcus raised his eyebrows.

Tom nodded.

"No, he didn't show them to me. But he said my investment was all documented. Dani did that, you know."

"Dani?"

"She wanted extra money for something, so Roy hired her to help with the paperwork."

Tom was genuinely surprised. "Did Pedro know about their arrangement?"

"I don't know."

Tom looked at Harvey. "Interesting."

"Do you need me for anything else?"

"No. Thank you for your cooperation."

Marcus walked away, and Tom said, "I guess she was really serious about that nose job."

"And she can keep a secret," Harvey said. "I wonder what else she knows."

Tom rubbed his chin. "Let's get some lunch before we tackle the Scotts. Perhaps you could let them know that we want to talk to them before they leave."

"Sure. Be right back."

Tom signaled the waitress and asked for menus while Harvey was gone. Service was quick since there were few customers in the middle of the day. Harvey returned, and they both ordered sandwiches and fries.

"This is the strangest case," Tom mumbled. "We circle round and round with no clear indication of guilt or innocence."

"Why do you think that is?"

Tom paused while the waitress delivered their lunch, then said, "Usually, when witnesses give you contrary information, the evidence disproves one or the other. This time it hasn't."

"Want me to get the Scotts?" Harvey asked.

"Yes. You can start by asking them about the water bottle."

Harvey returned to the table with Lizzie and Greg. Neither of them looked their best; stress was gnawing at everyone in *Torque*. Lizzie set the bar high, so a stranger might not notice her less-than-perfect hair and makeup and the red, sleep-deprived eyes. Greg followed her with rumpled khakis and razor stubble.

"Thank you for meeting with us," Harvey began. "I know this has been difficult for you, but we have a few more questions."

"We understand, detective," Greg managed.

"Could you think back to the day Cal died and try to remember what he did with his water bottle? I was told he had it at the Visitor's Center."

"Thank you. After you changed clothes, you rode to *Pastel Canyon*. Did anything unusual happen when you arrived at the turn out?"

"No..." Lizzie looked at Greg. "Well, one thing."

"Rachel pulled her bike in front of Cal's when they were parking, and both their bikes went over. Nothing serious, but Pedro went to help right them, and Rachel was making a fuss," Greg said.

"Did you see any bags or water bottles lying around?"

Greg shook his head. "I'm just not sure."

"Cal had a picture of a man named Anton who looked like he was threatening Lizzie. Can you tell us about that?"

Greg started with a frown. "Anton was here?"

"Y-yes." Lizzie looked down.

"Why didn't you tell me?"

"I didn't want you to worry." Lizzie let go of his hand and fluttered hers around. "Cal said he could take care of it. Then he tried to blackmail me once he figured out who I am."

Greg pressed his lips together and looked at the detectives. "I suppose you know who she is."

"Yes. Cal couldn't have had much leverage if your family already knew you were here," Harvey pointed out.

"True. Anton just happened to be in town, and he recognized me."

"What will we do now?" Greg asked, taking her hand once again.

"I don't know, but I'm tired of hiding. We need to meet with my father and make some kind of truce."

Tom cleared his throat. "Is there anything else we should know?"

"I think that's everything," Greg said. "Have you heard anything about the coins?"

"No. Were they insured?" Tom asked.

"Possibly, but I don't have access to Roy's paperwork."

"You could ask Cathy."

"He didn't confide in her. She didn't even know about the coins."

"Who told you that?"

Greg's eyebrows rose. "Marcus."

"He said you didn't actually show him the coins."

"That's true. I didn't know if I could trust him."

"And now?"

He shrugged. "Who knows? We're both out a small fortune."

Tom studied the Scotts and rubbed his chin. *Does he realize he's trying to steal from Cathy?*

Tom and Harvey stood. "Thank you both for your time." He stuck out his hand and shook Greg's, then Lizzie's.

After they left the bar, Tom said, "We need to find a way to get Rachel to open up."

"Maybe Sam has already talked to her," Harvey suggested.

Tom hesitated.

"What happened between you two?"

He shrugged and shook his head.

Harvey gaped as Tom walked away.

Chapter 24

Dinner that evening was back at Carlos 'N Charlie's, the restaurant where Sam had met Roy. She stood at the entrance and watched Greg and Lizzie get seated across from Pedro and Dani. They looked much as they had on Sam's first night, but they had changed. The relaxed, carefree spirit had been replaced with something else; Sam couldn't quite put her finger on it. Almost a feeling of foreboding. Even Marcus, who waved her over, wasn't quite himself.

Sadness washed over her as she joined the others and remembered that first evening. *It's probably better that Cathy isn't here.*

She took the seat next to Marcus and looked around. They were down to six. "I had shrimp tacos last time. You stole one!"

"To be fair, leaving them sitting in front of me for that long was cruel and unusual."

"You might have a point."

Greg cleared his throat. "Does anyone want to talk about what's going on?"

"I'm not sure if anyone has new information," Marcus said.

Everyone looked around silently.

"Is Cathy okay?" Lizzie asked.

"She's doing better," Sam said.

"How do you know?"

"I went to visit her."

Lizzie lowered her eyes. "I should have gone too."

No one at the table knew that Rachel had been taken to the hospital, so no one mentioned her.

"Does anyone want to continue with *Torque?*" Greg asked.

166

The Cardinal, The Fat Boy & The Flamingo

No one replied. "Better question. What are your plans after this?"

"I'm new, so it's possible no one cares, but I plan to go home," Sam said.

"I might stay in Vegas," Marcus said.

"We might stay with *Torque* if you do," Pedro said.

Greg nodded. "Lizzie and I are up for some more adventure. Anybody know about Cathy and Rachel?"

Sam shook her head. "I think Cathy has lost her enthusiasm, but I'm not sure what her plans are."

"Where is Rachel?" Dani asked. "I haven't seen her for a couple of days."

They all looked at each other and shrugged.

"I'll check on her after dinner," Sam said.

Greg and Pedro continued talking about destinations.

Marcus leaned in and whispered, "I wonder if she stole those coins and ran."

"Hard to say. Do you want to go with me to check on her after dinner?"

"Yeah."

"Why are you two always whispering?" Dani complained.

Sam looked at Marcus, and he shrugged.

Tom and Stewart were seated before *Torque* showed up. They ordered a simple dinner and kept their eyes on the somewhat subdued group.

Tom's phone rang while they were waiting for their food.

"Cork here."

"Yes?

"Thank you, Claire. I'll let him know."

He hung up and smiled at Stewart. "The gun is a match, and there are prints on the spade. Let's round 'em up after dinner. I see Sam leaving the table; maybe we can work out a plan."

Tom put down his napkin and walked quickly in the direction she was headed.

Sam excused herself to visit the ladies' room and ran into Tom, literally.

"Oof. Sorry! Tom?"

He hung his head sheepishly. "My fault, I think. I was trying to head you off."

They both chuckled.

"Could we spend some time together this evening?" he asked.

"Yes. I told the group I'd check on Rachel after dinner, and Marcus said he'd like to go too. Do you want to meet us upstairs?"

"Good idea. I'll head up after you do."

Dani had walked by while Sam and Tom were talking. She was waiting in the ladies' room when Sam finally got there. "What are you up to, Sam? Are you telling that cop everything we say, or are you just a playah?"

Sam raised one eyebrow. "Why are you always commenting on my love life? What does it matter to you?"

"Marcus isn't into you."

"I know that. We're friends. I just wonder why you keep commenting on it."

"Because I think you're up to something, and I want the others to notice too."

"What could I be up to? I thought you were really nice when we met. Since I've been here, though, you've told me we're not friends. You've told me to go home, and you said I'm up to something. You're clearly not as nice as I thought. You don't even try."

"Why should I? You came, you watched us go through hell, now you'll leave. Great vacation for you."

"I'm sorry you see it that way. I don't find death entertaining, Dani. And even if I don't know everyone as well as you do, I still feel a degree of loss and pain."

"The worst part is knowing the murderer is one of your friends. I want it to be you, but I know it's not."

Sam felt overcome by a wave of pity, and she hugged Dani hard. Surprisingly, Dani hugged her back. "I would change things if I could," Sam said.

"I know. I'm sorry."

They looked at each other with tears in their eyes and a new understanding between them. *We won't ever be best friends, but maybe we won't be enemies either.*

When they got back to the table, Pedro said, "I thought maybe you'd fallen in."

Dani tossed her hair and ignored him.

"Does anyone want to move to the bar?" Lizzie asked.

"Sam and I are going to check on Rachel," Marcus said.

"Maybe we should all go," Greg said.

Pedro looked at him. "Why?"

Greg looked at Marcus, then said, "She's still a member of *Torque*. We should make sure she's okay."

"Whatever, man. Let's go then."

They all left the restaurant together and headed for the elevators. Sam looked back at Tom and shrugged.

Tom watched *Torque* leave en masse and caught Sam's shrug. "Stewart, maybe you can swing by the reception desk and borrow an employee with a passkey. I'll follow them up."

He got on an elevator and arrived shortly after *Torque*. They were banging on the door and calling for Rachel when he got there.

"Hello, detective," Marcus said. "Why am I not surprised to see you?"

Everyone turned and watched him approach.

"What's going on here?" Tom asked.

"We wanted to check on Rachel," Sam said.

"We haven't seen her for a couple of days," Dani added.

Tom heard the ding of the elevator. "Luckily, we have a key."

169

He turned around to find Stewart and a security guard.

Tom watched as the guard opened the door for Stewart, and everyone filed in behind him. He noted that Lizzie and Dani were in a hurry to enter, followed by Marcus and Sam; Greg and Pedro hung back. *Do they think there's a body?*

Everyone looked around the tidy room.

"Where is she?" Lizzie asked.

"It doesn't look like she ran," Marcus said.

"Do any of you know where she is?" Tom asked.

They looked at each other and shook their heads.

"Let's all meet in the conference room downstairs tomorrow morning at 11am," Tom said. "We'll have breakfast and discuss what's been going on. Before you go, please stop at the door and let officer Brown take your fingerprints."

"Who's paying for breakfast," Stewart whispered.

"You are," Tom whispered back.

When everyone but Sam had gone, the captain agreed to take the prints back to the station, and the security guard locked up Rachel's room.

Tom walked up to Sam and put his hands on her shoulders. He gazed into her eyes. "I feel like there's something special between us, but ever since our breakfast at the bagel shop, I've felt you pulling away. I know I've been busy, but what happened?"

"I like you, Tom, and we have a lot of chemistry, but God has someone special in mind for me, and you're not the one."

"Is this about me not going to mass with you?"

Sam shrugged. "That was one of the signs. We can still be great friends, and you are still welcome to visit the ranch."

Tom put his arms around her waist and whispered, "Can I kiss you?"

It was oh so tempting, but Sam put her hands against his chest and shook her head. "I'm sorry, Tom, but we're just not meant to be."

"Even if I go to mass with you in the morning?"

"I think I have an idea."

"I keep dreaming of flamingos. They are supposed to mean you need to look at things from a different perspective. I thought it meant personally, but I am starting to think it's about the murders."

Tom tilted his head and looked at her with an odd expression on his face.

"We've been assuming that all of these events are about Marcus or Greg and the coins. What if they are about something else? What are the main motives for murder?"

"Love, revenge, greed?"

"Marcus had no reason to kill Roy unless he's lying about everything. Greg found out about the coins from Marcus, I think. Who might have killed for love or revenge?"

Tom's eyes got a faraway look.

"Think on it overnight. I will too. It's there waiting for us to see it."

Completely ignoring what Sam said earlier, he took her face and kissed her soundly. Then he stepped back, leaving her trembling. "Sorry. I couldn't help it," he mumbled. He turned and fled toward the staircase

Sam stood and watched him go. His kiss shook her to the core, but she knew he wasn't for her. She thought about it on her way back to her room, reliving that electricity he sparked. Somehow, she made her way back to her room and found herself on her knees once again.

"Father, I need your guidance. This trip has been so much more than I bargained for. I have learned a lot, especially about myself. But, Lord, the more I learn, the more I realize I don't know. Please help me follow your path and inspire Tom in his quest for truth. In the name of the father, the Son, and the Holy Ghost, amen."

Sam climbed into bed and fell asleep almost immediately.

Just before her alarm clock rang, Sam's eyes popped open, and she sat up. *Dani was working for Roy.*

171

Chapter 25

Tom was up most of the night, waiting for fingerprint results and working out the solution in his head. When he arrived at the Flamingo, Harvey had set everything up beautifully in one of the conference rooms. The simple buffet stretched along one side of the room, and a long, rectangular table was set up in the middle. The captain sat at one end. Tom would sit at the other. Harvey and a police officer would keep an eye on the proceedings.

Sam arrived first and hurried over to him, looking like she would burst.

He smiled. "You figured it out too."

She nodded vigorously.

"Without fingerprints."

Her mouth made an oh. "You have proof?"

"It might be a little circumstantial, but hopefully, we'll get a confession."

Sam let out a big breath. "Where should I sit?"

"Get some breakfast and sit here next to me. We'll see where everyone else decides to sit."

"I feel rude taking food before we start."

"Coffee, at least?"

"Okay. Twist my arm." She smiled.

Marcus arrived next and sat next to Sam, then Pedro and Dani entered the room. They sat to Stewart's right, on the opposite side of the table.

"Please help yourself to breakfast," Tom said.

Greg and Lizzie shuffled in, Lizzie taking the seat next to Dani.

Sam and Marcus served themselves from the buffet and returned to the table.

"That looks really good," Dani said, rising from her seat. The others followed her to the buffet and were getting re-seated when Cathy and Rachel walked in.

All speech and movement stopped for an instant before everyone tried to speak at once.

"Please get some breakfast, ladies, and we'll begin."

"Is this the gathering where the great detective reveals all?" Greg rolled his eyes.

"Something like that. Aren't you curious?" Stewart asked.

"Who are you?" Pedro asked.

"My apologies," Tom said. "This is Captain White of the LVPD."

Cathy sat next to Stewart on his left and smiled up at him. Rachel sat quietly next to her.

Tom was a little nervous. He wasn't much for public speaking, and he didn't like being the center of attention. He cleared his throat. "Let's begin. We have a lot of ground to cover. I met all of you, the members of Torque, when your leader was shot and killed in his hotel room. The scene of the crime seemed confusing because of the clues left behind. We made note of them and set out to interview all of you. What we found was that none of you had an airtight alibi except Sam."

"What about me?" Cathy asked. "I was with Sam."

"That was only airtight if he died after you left your room."

Cathy stared at him with wide eyes. "You thought I could have killed him?"

"It was a possibility." Tom shrugged. "The second murder was death by anaphylactic shock, which caused the victim to fall from a great height. It is impossible to tell which actually caused his death, but together they were fatal."

"What is that? *Anafatic* shock?" Dani asked.

"He had a severe allergic reaction. Someone put milk in his water bottle."

Dani's eyes got very round, and she looked at Pedro and then back at Tom. "That's why he fell?"

"Yes." Tom noticed that Dani and Rachel had tears in their eyes. Greg's lips were pressed together, and his scowl appeared permanent. Tom didn't look at Sam. "The window of opportunity was small. The victim had his water bottle at the Visitor's Center. It must have been swapped with the bottle of milk sometime before he went over the edge. Rachel, what happened when you parked at *Pastel Canyon?*"

She looked down and fiddled with her bacon. "I was being petty. I was mad at him because he was trying to blackmail me, so I tried to take his parking spot. He stopped too slowly and bumped into me, and both our bikes tipped over."

"What was he trying to blackmail you about?"

"A photo he had of me and a man."

"Did anyone help you with your bikes?"

"Yes, Pedro came over and helped, then Greg."

"That was nice of them." Tom smiled slightly. "Up on the *Fire Wave*, Cal put his bottle down briefly, then picked it up and drank from it. Rachel, you were the only person near him."

Rachel shrunk back, and Pedro sneered.

"That doesn't mean you swapped the bottles; it only narrows the window even more if you didn't."

Rachel's body uncoiled slightly. "One other person could have done it," she said.

"I already told him I went back for my cap," Marcus said.

"Did you tell him that you found Cal's forgotten water bottle and trotted it up to him?"

Tom stared at him. "Pretty big omission."

Marcus looked down.

"Then came the great coin fiasco. Roy had a business buying and selling rare coins. Marcus showed up and asked to be part of the business."

"He asked *me* to come."

174

"According to two witnesses, he did *not* ask you to come and was not sure if you were *actually* his nephew."

Marcus frowned. "Roy could be really weird sometimes. He knew I was his nephew. We spent summers and holidays together every year of my life until he married Cathy. I knew him *very* well."

"Who told you that he kept secrets from Cathy and was going to divorce her?"

"Greg did."

"Who told Greg about the coins?"

Greg smiled.

"I guess I did when I broke into his room looking for them," Marcus admitted.

"What does this have to do with the rest of us?" Dani whined. "I'm bored."

"Go get some more coffee," Pedro suggested.

Lizzie was looking at Greg. "What did you do?"

"Nothing." Greg took a bite of bacon.

"Greg visited Rachel and offered her a cut of the coins if she would take a Valium and skip dinner. He took an extra to give Cathy, thereby removing Lizzie from the scene," Tom said. "Since Rachel wouldn't be at dinner, the imaginary coin theft could be blamed on her."

"Wait!" Marcus stood. "What do you mean by imaginary?"

"Please sit back down. Greg never had the coins. He thought staging a theft might flush out the person who did have them."

"What does this have to do with the murders?" Lizzie asked.

"Well, two things. First, Cathy got nervous and decided to talk. And second, the murderer decided since Rachel had already taken a Valium, they could help her take a bunch more."

"How did the murderer know?" Greg asked.

"She told him."

Rachel stared at Pedro, who was no longer sneering.

Questions started coming from all directions until Tom held up a hand.

175

"Dani was secretly working for Roy to earn money for a personal project. Her job was documenting the purchase and sale of the coins."

"I didn't do anything wrong!" Tears sprouted from Dani's eyes. "I didn't even get paid for the last week because he died!" She turned her face and pressed it against Pedro's chest. He put his arm around her.

"Pedro is a jealous man. Since Dani didn't want him to know about her job, all he knew was that she was spending a lot of time in Roy's hotel room."

Dani's head popped up, and she scooted away with wide eyes. "You didn't!"

"Of course not."

"I don't know exactly how it happened, but we have evidence that proves it did. Pedro went to Roy's suite to confront him."

Harvey and the police officer had been gradually moving to position themselves between Pedro and the exit.

"He used Roy's own gun to shoot him twice in the chest. We weren't able to find the gun and didn't know why the air conditioner was turned up so high, but when Pedro broke the glass on Roy's watch, he left a little pile of soil."

"This is ridiculous," Pedro said, crossing his arms. "I had an alibi."

"The evidence doesn't lie. We found a potted plant on the patio. The gun was buried in the pot, and the small spade he used had Pedro's fingerprint on it. When we were retrieving the pot, the hot air from outside noticeably warmed the room. That's why he turned up the A/C. He didn't want to call attention to the patio."

Cathy was inconsolable. Her face was mottled, and her eyes and nose ran. "You killed my Roy because he gave Dani a job?"

"I didn't kill anyone!" Pedro yelled. Stewart placed his hand on Pedro's shoulder, and he shrugged it off.

"When you first arrived in Las Vegas, you had a little tryst with Rachel. Cal had pictures.

I suspect he also caught you coming out of Roy's room. He tried to blackmail Rachel, but she had less to lose than you did. There was no way Dani could see those photos. Cal had to go."

"You're crazy. Why would I mess around with a dog like her when I have Dani?"

"*Had* might be more accurate. You killed Roy because you thought we were having an affair, but you were the one HAVING THE AFFAIR!" Dani stood and picked up her fork, stabbing at him with it.

Harvey pulled her away from Pedro.

Rachel narrowed her eyes.

"You play a dangerous game, *amor*, publicly insulting your lover who can easily out you."

"It's true," Dani said. "You have some easily identifiable equipment."

"The last attempted murder was Rachel. She was a loose end. She called Pedro and told him about Greg's deal, letting him know she wouldn't be at dinner. The opportunity was too good to be true. Pedro stopped by Rachel's room and forced the remaining Valium into her mouth. Fortunately, she threw them up after he left, and Sam thought to check on her after dinner."

"How do you know Greg didn't give her all the Valium?" Marcus asked. "Sorry old man, but it's a valid question."

"When he clamped her mouth shut, she couldn't breathe, and she clawed at his arms. The doctor found skin particles under her fingernails. Would you like to roll up your sleeves, Pedro?"

Pedro stood abruptly. "I don't know what you're playing at, but I don't have to sit here and take this."

"That's true," Tom said. "Would you like to read him his rights, Detective Brother?"

Pedro swung around and tried to shove Harvey out of the way, but he was too late. The police officer restrained Pedro as Harvey said, "Pedro Nunez, I'm arresting you for the murders of Roy Williams and Cal Lenox and the attempted murder of

Rachel Simon. You have the right to remain silent..."

Pedro fought against Harvey and the handcuffs, not listening to the recitation of his rights. He twisted and kicked and even tried to bite him once.

Everyone was silent as Harvey continued, but Tom could see the deep sadness and horror in their faces. There wasn't a dry eye in the room other than the police. Even Greg, who was the gruffest and most stoic of the group, had suspiciously watery eyes. He cleared his throat and made a show of comforting Lizzie. Tom had watched Dani move farther and farther away from Pedro until she stood on the other side of Lizzie. Cathy got up and approached her as they led Pedro from the room. She put her arms around her, and they sobbed together silently.

Sam sat very still, her face contorting in a way that told Tom she was struggling to retain her composure. She held Marcus' hand tightly. He had put his other arm around Rachel, who was crying into his chest. Tom was at a loss and was thankful when Sam stood and began to speak.

"Let's all take a moment to pray for our lost friends and family," she said. She closed her eyes and said, 'Dear heavenly father, please take care of Roy and Cal; welcome them into your eternal embrace. And Lord, please give us peace and help us to heal from all the damage and loss we've experienced. Help us to lean on you and each other for solace in our time of grief. In the name of the Father, the Son, and the Holy Ghost.'" Sam crossed herself and sat down. The rest of *Torque* remained with their eyes closed for a moment, then hugged and whispered amongst themselves.

Tom sat next to Sam. "That was nice. Thank you for rescuing me up there."

She gave him a sad smile and leaned her head on his shoulder. "Things like this are so hard to understand; how someone can decide that their wants are more important than others' lives."

Finally, Greg said, "Let's have dinner tonight and decide what we will do next. Dani, I hope you'll join us. Sam too."

He took Lizzie's hand and slowly left the room. Rachel linked arms with Dani, and they left as well.

Cathy approached with a bag and set it on the table in front of Marcus. "Can we talk?"

Marcus' eyebrows went up, but he nodded and stood.

"I'm sorry I doubted you. I don't know what happened between you and Roy, but the coins you invested in are in this bag with his and mine. He had Dani document everything."

Marcus let out a deep breath. "Thank you. This is such a relief. Have you had them this whole time?"

"Roy told me to put them in the main hotel safe when we arrived. Someone should probably call Greg on his attempt to steal them, but we've all had enough trauma for a lifetime."

Marcus pulled a letter out of his pocket and handed it to Cathy. "I was going to show you this."

Cathy took the letter and unfolded it. It was old and tattered and looked like it might have been read many times.

Dear Marcus, I just recently heard about your parents and am sorry I couldn't be there for you. I am probably the worst uncle in history, but I didn't want to get Cathy involved in our strange family dynamic, and we have been moving around a lot. I don't know what else to say other than I really am sorry. Since we have always been close and I don't have children of my own, I would like you to join us and take over the family business one day. Please give me a call, and I'll tell you more so you can make an informed decision. I haven't told anyone about you or the business, so I'd like you to keep our relationship under your hat for now. Looking forward to hearing from you, Uncle Roy

Cathy read the note, then she read it again. "Roy was such a strange bird. Why wouldn't he want me to meet his family? *Your* family?

I thought our little secrets were our own special little joke, but it seems like he played that game with other people too." She handed the note to Sam, who looked at it and handed it to Tom.

"We lived out in the countryside. My parents drank and smoked a lot of pot. Sometimes they were… frustrating. Roy usually came to visit me, not them. He took me camping and swimming." Marcus shrugged. "I always thought he was the father I should have had." He looked at Cathy. "He didn't want you to meet them. He was ashamed."

Cathy's mouth turned down, and her eyes got suspiciously moist. "He did a lot of compartmentalizing. I know he loved me, and it sounds like he loved you too." She shook her head. "So many secrets."

Sam gave her a side hug. "Marcus and I have decided to be honorary siblings, so I guess you now have a nephew by marriage and an honorary niece."

Cathy's tears finally spilled onto her cheeks, and she smiled. "I love that! Can I be part of your honorary family, Marcus?"

"Of course, Aunt Cathy." He hugged her too.

"Will the two of you be joining the others at dinner?" Sam asked.

"Yes, let's. We've lost so much; let's keep our friends. You come too, Sam."

"At Benihana, right?"

"Yes. Six o'clock. See you then." She hugged them both again before she left.

"I guess we're going too," Sam said to Marcus as they watched Cathy float out of the room.

"Yeah. I might bring Darren. I'll see you tonight, sis." He gave her a wink.

When it was just Tom and Sam again, he asked, "Would you like to go on a little road trip tomorrow? Just you and me?"

"Can we go somewhere where there's water?"

"Kayaking sound good?"

The Cardinal, The Fat Boy & The Flamingo

Sam's eyes lit up. "Kayaking sounds great!"

"I'll pick you up in the parking garage at nine."

Sam arrived at Benihana's alone that evening. She was shown into a semi-private room that Greg had reserved the previous week. Since she was early, she ordered a Japanese beer and sat down at the end of the table. Marcus and Darren peeked around the corner and waved. *They look so happy. I'm glad Marcus wasn't a bad guy.* She smiled as they approached.

"Don't *you* look delicious!" Darren said with a grin. "What are you doing in here, all by yourself?"

"Just waiting for you-u," she sang.

Marcus covered his ears. "Do not quit your day job!"

"Pft!" She swatted at him playfully.

Cathy, Rachel, and Dani walked in together. Sam was glad they were supporting each other. Greg and Lizzie were right behind. Everyone appeared to be cautiously optimistic.

"Watching the food preparation is part of the fun at Benihana's, so maybe we'll talk about our plans after we eat," Greg said.

"Good idea!" Cathy said.

Their chef joined them, and the show began. Sam had never been to a teppanyaki restaurant before. She was amazed by the lightning speed and skill of the chef and amused by his jokes and little tricks. "Watching him prepare the food somehow makes it taste even better," she whispered to Marcus.

"Do you want me to get you his phone number?" Marcus winked.

"No." She blushed.

After everyone had eaten more than they should have, the chef excused himself, and Greg said, "I don't know how everyone else is feeling, but Lizzie and I are ready to ride. Vegas has lost some of its appeal. I'm not sure I'll ever want to come back."

"This was always a special place for Roy and me. I don't know how to hold onto the memories without reliving the nightmare."

181

"It will take some time," Sam said.

Cathy nodded. "For now, Rachel, Dani, and I are thinking about getting a place in Florida. Do you want to ride out there with us?"

Greg looked at Lizzie, whose eyes lit up at the idea. "I guess maybe we do." He chuckled.

Lizzie smiled wider than Sam had ever seen.

"How about you, Marcus?"

Marcus looked at Darren. "I'm going to stick around Vegas for a while."

"Would you like to come with us, Sam?" Cathy asked.

"I would, but I think I need to get home. I was running away from my feelings when I left, but I've realized that I can't do that. My feelings just go with me." Sam laughed at herself. "I've enjoyed getting to know all of you, and I'd love to join you again sometime. If you'll have me."

"Sure," Dani said. "Whenever you have to get away from that stinky ranch." She wrinkled her nose, and everyone laughed.

Cathy had tears in her eyes. "I'm going to miss you, Sam."

"We'll visit. And we can share pictures. I've never been to Florida."

"I get to visit your ranch sometime, right?" Marcus asked.

"Of course. All of you are welcome whenever you like."

"I have a vacation coming up." Darren winked.

"You too, Darren."

The evening morphed into a farewell party. Sam felt at peace when she returned to her room. "I think they will heal together now. And we will meet again. Thank you, Father, for bringing us together. Thank you for Cathy and her words of wisdom. Thank you for this opportunity to learn and grow. Please look after all of them. Bring them peace and joy." Sam crossed herself and got into bed. She saw Tom's face in her mind's eye and smiled as sleep took her.

Chapter 26

Tom was waiting in the parking garage at nine, as promised. The Emerald Cove kayak tour provided transportation, but he and Sam thought it would be more fun to take their bikes. "Ready to head out?"

Sam grinned. "I can't wait. Lead the way!"

They couldn't talk as they rode, but Sam was mesmerized by the desert and the many types of rock formations. *Even in the midst of this harsh, desolate land, there is incredible beauty, like Santo Milagro. I wonder what Emerald Cove is like.*

They reached Willow Beach Marina in a little less than an hour. The bus was just behind them, so they shed their outer layers and were ready to greet their group when they arrived.

"I have a dry bag if there's anything you want to bring, Tom."

"Maybe just my keys." He tossed them over.

"Need any sunscreen?"

"Yes. Good idea."

They sprayed each other and went to meet the others.

The guide was a funny guy. Sam thought he might have missed his calling as a stand-up comic. His safari hat covered any hair he might have, and he had the bushiest eyebrows Sam had ever seen. Dressed in white and orange, knee-length swim trunks and a bright orange tank top. Sam thought he was very theatrical. *He belongs in Hollywood.*

"Hello, everyone," he said. "I'm Andre, and I'll be your guide today. Have any of you been kayaking before?"

Several hands went up, including Tom's.

Andre rubbed his hands together and grinned.

"Good. You will be in charge of coaching and safety today since this is my first time too."

He waited for a little stir of panic before chuckling. "Just kidding. Let's get you all fitted for your kayaks, then we'll go over some basics." He walked over to Sam and removed his sunglasses. "Would you like to ride with me?"

"No, sir." She grinned. "I want the full experience."

"I can't say I'm not disappointed, but that's the true sign of an adventurer." He winked.

Tom scowled a little.

"We will kayak four miles out and back with two, fifteen-minute breaks, including a short hike to a bluff above the river. Does everyone have a current last will and testament?" The group tittered nervously, and Andre chuckled. "Everyone, put on your life vests, and let's head out!"

After they got used to maneuvering their kayaks, the group was able to make good time. Andre engaged them with information about local history and pointed out wildlife along the banks of the river. Break time was used to swim around and take pictures.

As they approached Emerald Cove, they gazed in awe at the stunning color of the water. Other groups were ahead of them, but they chatted and admired the view while they waited.

By the time they returned to the marina, Sam was pretty tired. Tom helped her pull her kayak out of the water. "Did you enjoy the tour?"

"It was amazing!" Sam grinned.

"Did you bring a towel?"

"Yes. Did you?"

Tom nodded. "Let's see about getting changed, then I have a little surprise."

Sam danced around a little. "A surprise!"

They said goodbye to Andre and the rest of their group and headed for the restrooms.

The Cardinal, The Fat Boy & The Flamingo

After they were changed, they sat at a picnic table, and Tom fished out two small cooler boxes from his saddle bags. Handing one to Sam, he said, "Bon appetit."

Opening hers, Sam's mouth formed into an oh. She gave it a sniff and sighed deeply. Inside was chilled barbecue. Sam took a bite and chewed happily. Tender ribs and chicken, potato salad, coleslaw, and biscuits. "This is delicious. Thank you, Tom."

"Sorry I couldn't keep it warm."

"It's probably better this way since it's so hot outside."

They ate in silence for a few minutes, then Tom said, "I know you're leaving for home tomorrow. Can we stay in touch? I'd like to see you again."

"Yes," Sam said quietly. "Perhaps you can come out for Thanksgiving."

"That sounds great. I'll ask for time off when we get back to town. I wanted to drive back with you, but I didn't know when to request time. The case drew out longer than I expected."

"It did. Great job, by the way."

"You, too. How did you figure it out?"

"I don't know. I woke up in the morning with *Dani worked for Roy* in my head."

"I was waiting for fingerprints."

"We came to the same conclusion."

Tom nodded. "Ready to head back?"

"Yes. Thank you for today. I think this has been my best day here."

"It has been one of my best as well."

They rode back to Las Vegas and parted ways at the Flamingo. *I wish I knew what I was doing. This feels very wrong.* She gave Tom a hug and watched him ride off.

The next morning Sam's heart was heavy as she checked out of her room and prepared to leave. She had already said goodbye to Tom and the remaining members of *Torque*, but it felt wrong.

185

She swung her saddlebags over her bike and prepared to mount when the deep growl of an approaching bike distracted her. Tom stopped his bike and dismounted, walking toward her with purpose. He gathered her up in his arms and hugged her tight. "I took the time off. I'm coming with you if it's okay."

Sam hugged him back and the weight lifted. "It's very okay. I'm glad you're coming."

Tom let out a deep breath. "Good. Ready to go?"

"Now, I am," Sam said with a grin.

Chapter 27

The ride back to New Mexico seemed to fly by. Even though they couldn't talk while they were riding, Sam enjoyed Tom's presence and looked forward to their stops. Each time they stopped, Tom asked around and discovered interesting local sights and activities: an ice cream shop, a lovely hike, a festival. In the evening, they talked for hours over dinner.

The first night Sam asked Tom how he ended up being a detective.

"All of the men in my family have been in either law enforcement or the clergy. It goes back generations. I'm not very scholarly, so I chose a life of adventure."

"Do you love it?"

Tom looked into her eyes for a long moment. "You always surprise me," he said with a soft smile. "Do you know that no one has ever asked me that?"

"Well? Do you?"

"That's a difficult question. I can't imagine doing anything else. I enjoy solving the puzzle and seeing justice served."

"But?"

"It's a trade off. It's my life, I guess. My work, or my work habits perhaps, cost me my marriage. I am always surrounded by the worst of humanity, and my best friend is my captain. You are the first person I've connected with outside of work in five years."

"You don't look very old. How long ago were you married?"

"I got married and entered the police academy when I was eighteen. The marriage lasted three years. She left while I was at work and took my dog. I've been working non-stop ever since."

Sam put her hand on his and smiled. "Perhaps it's time for a vacation."

"I think you're right. Now it's your turn. Do you love being a rancher?"

"I love Santo Milagro and the ranch, but I'm not really a hands-on rancher, so I've been lonely and bored since my father passed away. I've been trying to think of something I can do that will be fulfilling, something I can feel passionate about."

"What are your favorite things to do?"

"I like to be outdoors. I like swimming and riding my horse. I like showing people things, like plants, animal tracks, cooking over a fire…"

"Have you ever thought about survival training?"

"Taking a class?"

"Well, you might want to take a certification class, but I mean running your own survival camps. That way, you can be outdoors, meet new people, and teach them how to survive in the wilderness."

Sam rolled the idea around in her head. "You could be right. I think I might enjoy that. Thank you."

"Want to take a little after-dinner walk?"

Sam nodded, and when he took her hand, she felt the same frisson of electricity she felt the night they walked along the strip. *I wonder if he feels it too.*

Tom was feeling all kinds of things, and after kissing Sam goodnight at her door, he spent the night tossing and turning. Morning couldn't come soon enough. He was waiting in the dining room when she arrived. "Ready for another day of exploring?"

"Absolutely! Just let me grab some coffee."

Tom grinned.

"Priorities, my man."

"Your man?"

"Yeah, like Lollie Sharp would say it." Sam laughed.

"Can we leave Lollie out of it? I'd like to be your man."

188

The Cardinal, The Fat Boy & The Flamingo

"I think you already are."

"Glad we got that straight. Now let me find you some coffee before you change your mind!" Tom felt almost lightheaded with her admission. He had realized the night before that he loved her. Not an easy-going, just for now kind of love, but the *I can't live without her* kind.

Tom handed her two cups of coffee and said he had a call to make. "I'll be back in a few. Go ahead and get caffeinated."

"Thanks! Maybe I'll give Roger a call while I wait."

"Who's Roger?"

"He's the head ranch hand. He's looking after things while I'm gone. I should let him know we'll be there tomorrow."

"Good idea." Tom gave her a quick kiss on the lips and moved out of hearing to make his call.

Once they were on the road, the miles seemed to stretch forever. It was a long day, but the second stop had a pool. Sam was practically hopping up and down with excitement. She loved water, whether it was a lake, a river, or a swimming pool. She didn't really understand Tom's nonchalant attitude but happily splashed around by herself until he couldn't stay away. He waded in until he was behind her and then put one arm around her middle and touched her right shoulder blade with his other hand. "Is this your new tattoo?"

"Yes, didn't you see it when we went kayaking?"

"I guess I didn't see you from behind. What does it mean?"

"It's a cardinal and a crow; my cousin and I."

"You haven't told me much about him, but you must be close."

"I'll tell you about him at dinner, okay? Right now, I want to play in the water."

"Deal."

They arranged to meet in the hotel restaurant after they showered and changed. When Sam entered the dining room, she was a little surprised at the understated elegance.

Cozy booths and small tables gleamed in the soft light of chandeliers. The wait staff wore formal-looking black and white uniforms and carried food on shiny silver trays. Sam stopped and looked around. Tom caught her eye as he stood and pulled out a chair for her. *He's always so sweet and considerate.* Sam walked over and took her seat. "We're a little underdressed."

"It's okay. They are used to all kinds of people passing through." Tom smiled. "Would you like something to drink? I think I saw a strawberry margarita on the menu."

"Mm. Hard to say no to that."

They ordered margaritas and fajitas from an elderly waiter. He reminded Sam of an upper-crust butler. She had never met an upper-crust butler, but she had seen them in the movies.

When their food arrived, Tom reminded Sam that she promised to tell him about Jack. She started out telling him the same thing she had told Roy but was unsure how much she should say.

"So, Jack is your only living relative," Tom prompted. "I guess you got close since you got a tattoo of the two of you?"

"We did. I wanted him to stay, but he had to get back to his job."

"He's the medical examiner."

"Yes." She took a deep breath. "After he left, I found my father's journals and found out that we're not actually related by blood."

Tom blinked. "Did that affect your relationship?"

"I don't know. I haven't seen him since then."

"You love him." It wasn't a question.

"Yes, of course. He's my cousin. But he's not my cousin." Sam tilted her head a little. "It's confusing."

"If he moved to Santo Milagro and asked you to marry him, would you?"

"I don't know. I don't think so. We're not in that kind of place. Anyway, he told me he can't give up his position, so it's a moot point."

Tom nodded.

"Do you have family?"

"Yes. My parents, grandparents, siblings, aunts, uncles, and cousins all live in Colorado."

Sam's mouth made an oh.

"I never see them, though. I am always working, and they don't travel."

"I always wanted a big family," Sam said wistfully. "Sometimes the big families around Santo Milagro have fiestas. It's so much fun to see them singing and dancing and barbecuing together."

"My family's gatherings are not that fun." Tom grimaced.

"Do you think it's worse not to have any family or to have one you never see?"

"It's worse not to have any."

"Why?"

"Because if you have family, they are always there, whether or not you see them often."

Sam nodded slowly.

"We could make our own little family," Tom suggested.

Sam's eyebrows lifted. "Would you want to do that?"

He took her hands in his. "I think I might. I've fallen quite in love with you."

Sam smiled. "We will have to have a talk with Father Garcia while you're in town."

"Do we have to?"

"Don't you believe in God?"

"I do. I was raised Catholic. It's just that when my wife divorced me, our parish priest basically said I wasn't welcome anymore. I haven't been back since."

Sam looked at him in horror. "How terrible. Now I know you have to meet Father Garcia. He always tells me that we are only human and that God hears our prayers no matter where we pray. You will love him. Everyone does."

Tom's eyes sparkled. "You are something else. If you trust Father Garcia, then so do I." He kissed her knuckles. "Ready to call it a night?"

"Yes. It's been a long day."

The third day they were on the road early and planned to stop in Las Rodillas for lunch. When they pulled up to Mary's Diner, Tom said, "You like surprises, right?"

"Y-yeah... sometimes."

"Close your eyes." He took her hand. "No peeking."

Sam's lips curved up slightly as she let him lead her inside the diner.

"Ok. You can open your eyes."

"Surprise!" shouted the members of *Torque*.

"What?" Sam put her hand on her chest. "I can't believe it."

"We decided since we were coming in this direction anyway, we wanted to see your stinky ranch." Dani laughed.

Sam swiped at her tears as she hugged all of them. "I'm so glad you came!"

She got to Marcus and said, "I thought you were staying in Vegas."

"Tom pointed out he could use company on the way back."

"Now, if you'd stop your blubbering, I'm getting hungry," Greg huffed.

"Of course. Sorry, sir!" Sam grinned. "We can't have a hangry leader."

They all laughed and sat down to order.

Chapter 28

Aftr lunch, Sam and Tom led the formation to the ranch. When they pulled into the drive, Roger was outside brushing Ghost. Ghost stood very still, looking intently at Sam and whinnying loudly when Sam got off her bike, threw down her helmet, and ran toward her. She threw her arms around Ghost's neck and hugged her tight. "I missed you so much." Ghost nuzzled her back and snorted.

Finally, Sam looked up and saw Roger smiling at her. "Hi, Roger. I missed you too." She introduced everyone. "We might have to be creative about the sleeping arrangements. I'll give you guys a tour."

"Would you like me to go into town and get some supplies, Ms. Sam? We could barbecue."

"That would be great, Roger. Would you wait just a moment with Ghost? I think I should probably take her for a little ride before I do much else."

Roger nodded, and Sam took the group into the house.

Sam gave the standard tour, but it almost felt new since she had been away for a while. She showed everyone the kitchen, living room, and game room downstairs then led them upstairs. "Marcus, you can sleep here," she indicated the farthest bedroom, the one with what Jack called the *magic closet*. "If you need any cowboy duds, check the closet."

They passed to the next room, and Sam said, "Rachel, you can sleep in this room. This is my room," she said as they continued down the hall. "And this last room was my father's. Greg, you and Lizzie can sleep in here."

"Where will we sleep?" Dani asked.

193

"I'm going to let you two share the giant pull-out sofa. I hope you don't mind." Sam smiled.

"That sounds swell," Cathy said. "It will be like a pajama party."

"Leave it to you to find the fun. Do you have popcorn?"

"I'll have Roger put it on the list."

"Woot!" Dani yelled.

Marcus stuck his head out of his room. "Where is Tom going to sleep?"

Sam blushed. "He can bunk with me."

"What if he doesn't want to?"

"Then he can have your room, and you can sleep in the barn."

Everyone laughed, including Tom.

"Is it okay if I go into town with Roger?" he asked.

"Sure." She walked to the door with him. "Is everyone okay for half an hour? I need to take my horse for a ride."

A chorus of "yes" followed, so she strode out of the house and mounted Ghost in a single leap. She gave Tom and Roger a wave, then neatly jumped the fence and took off across the paddock at a gallop.

"Wow," was all Tom said.

"Yep. That about covers it. Ready to go?"

Tom stood staring after Sam for a few moments. He knew she was a rancher, and he could see that she was long and lean, but he had not expected that level of athleticism. He was fascinated.

"Tom, right? Are you ready?"

Tom shook his head. "What? Yes. Sorry. That was amazing."

"She and Ghost have some kind of weird connection. They are like family."

"No wonder she wanted to get back." Tom smiled.

"What do you do for a living?" Roger asked.

"I'm a police detective. I've never even been on a horse before."

"Sam will take care of that." Roger chuckled.

The two of them stopped at the small market in town to get meat and beer, then Roger drove down the street to the Sheriff's station and took Tom in to meet Mick. He walked in and obnoxiously hit the bell - ding ding ding - until Anita bustled out looking perturbed. "Roger! You stop that."

"Hello Anita." Roger grinned. "Is Mick around?"

"I think so. Let me go see."

She came back with Mick in tow. "Hey, Roger. What's up?"

"Hi, Mick. I just wanted to introduce you to Sam's friend, Tom. He's a detective from Las Vegas."

"We spoke on the phone." Tom smiled.

Mick stuck out his hand and shook Tom's. "A detective, huh? We could use a few of you. Ever thought about transferring to New Mexico?"

"Not until recently." Tom smiled. "You have an opening?"

"We always have openings. You should apply. There are times of drought and times of 24/7, but they somehow even out. Plus, you get to really know your community. It's a good place to live."

"I'll keep it in mind."

"Sam's back, obviously, and we're having a barbecue at the ranch. You should come, Mick."

"I'll stop by if I can. Thanks."

They waved to Anita on the way out the door and headed back to the ranch.

Sam had finished her ride and opened the pool. Tom found her sitting quietly by herself, watching everyone enjoying themselves. "Are you okay?" he asked.

"Yes. I was just remembering the last time I had lots of company and how I felt when everyone left."

"When Jack left."

"That too."

"And you think you will feel like that again."

Sam nodded unhappily.

"It will be different this time."

"What makes you think so?"

"Well, for one thing, you have a new project. And for another, I will be pestering you every day. I'll call or text or Skype. Okay?"

"I'll miss you, though."

"I'll miss you too, but we'll work something out. Tomorrow, we'll go visit Father Garcia, and Mick told me I should apply for a job here."

"You would hate it." Sam laughed. "The case of the missing cow!"

"Didn't you tell me there was a double homicide earlier this year?"

"Yes, but that was so rare that Mick had to ask Jack for help. Maybe you could apply in Las Rodillas. That's a little bigger town."

"We'll see, but you know what I mean. We have possibilities."

"Thanks, Tom. You always know just what to say."

"Changing the subject just a little, your horsemanship knocked my socks off. Where did you learn how to do that?"

"Do what? Ride? I've been on a horse since I could walk."

"Not just that. You sprung up on Ghost like a rocket, then jumped over the fence with no saddle or anything. It was incredible."

Sam blushed. "I don't know. I've been doing that for years. The only time I use a saddle on Ghost is when I'm camping and have a lot of supplies. She knows what I want her to do almost before I do."

"I was very impressed. Can you teach me to ride?"

"We can go out for a while tomorrow, if you want."

"That sounds fun. Now you enjoy your party, okay?"

"Right. Barbecue."

"I think Roger is already on it."

"Music then. And beer." Sam jumped up and turned on the cd player, then started passing out drinks. Mick arrived, and she ran to greet him. "Mick! You came! I've missed you."

He hugged her tight and kissed her cheek. "I've missed you too. Are these the bikers you met in Las Rodillas?"

"Yes. We had a little adventure in Vegas."

"So, I heard. I'm glad you're okay, and I'm glad you're home."

"Thanks. Me too. Vegas is not for me... except maybe the strawberry margaritas. That is now my favorite drink."

"That drink would give me hives." He smiled and winked.

His words reminded her of Cal and she froze, remembering the day at the *Fire Wave*.

"Hey," Mick said gently. He put his hand on her shoulder. "Are you alright?"

Sam blinked rapidly and stood up straighter. "I'm okay. Just don't make fun of my margaritas."

Mick smiled at her gently. "I'm here if you want to talk about it."

"I know. Thank you."

They walked over to where Roger was flipping burgers, and soon everyone was clamoring for food.

Once the party died down and everyone was settling in for the night, Tom said, "Are you sure it's okay if I sleep in your room?"

"I'd like to snuggle up with you and feel you close before you leave. We can control ourselves, can't we?"

"I'm not sure. You are pretty tempting," Tom said with a grin. "I'm just kidding. Well, I am, and I'm not, but we won't do anything you don't want to do. I am happy to snuggle."

"Good. I didn't want to send Marcus to the barn."

Tom chuckled and put his arms around her waist, attempting to kiss her.

"Nope. Better not do that right now. Go get your pjs on."

The next morning, after a big breakfast, everyone rode into Santo Milagro to look around. Sam wanted to visit the church and told the others they could meet at the Ugly Orange Cafe for lunch.

Strolling down Santo Milagro's one main street with Tom, Sam pointed out the main shops and businesses.

"It's impressive that you have a bank and a post office in such a small town," he said.

"Most of the businesses here were established to serve the ranching community. There are ranches for miles, even though the town itself is small."

"I see."

"You would be surprised if you saw the size of a local wedding. People have to stand outside the church!"

Tom's easy smile turned to something like alarm. Smoke was billowing out of one of the shops. "What's that? Is there a fire?"

"No, that's incense from my friend Melissa's shop. She might stop by later with my cats. There's the church up ahead."

Tom saw what looked like a modest, adobe-style church, but he could see a stained-glass window and a bell tower as well. His feet started dragging as they got closer. Sam surprised him again. "It will be okay." She squeezed his hand.

Tom felt a sense of familiarity when they passed through the heavy doors into the dimly lit interior of the church. He also felt a deep sense of inadequacy. A small, elderly man with a cap of gray, wind-swept curls approached them with a smile. "Samantha. It's so good to see you. We have missed you."

"I've missed you too, Father. I got back yesterday and wanted to introduce you to Tom."

"Hello, Tom. It's very good to meet you."

"Do you think you could talk to Tom about something that happened to him in the past before you speak to us as a couple?"

"Of course! Come with me, Tom."

Tom felt frozen to the floor, but Sam's soft smile gave him courage. He followed Father Garcia into his study.

Sam knelt in one of the pews. She wasn't worried about Tom because she knew Father Garcia well. He was a kind, gentle man, and he understood what it meant to be human.

"Dear Lord," she prayed, "thank you for bringing Tom into my life. Whether or not he is the man you have chosen for me, I have learned from him, and Father Garcia can help him find you again. I love him, but I will follow the path you have chosen for me. Thy will be done." Sam crossed herself and sat to wait.

Father Garcia came out smiling and asked her to join Tom and him. When they entered the study, Tom looked like it had been an emotional meeting. Father Garcia took his seat and looked from one to the other. "I understand that the two of you have fallen in love and are thinking of ways you can be together. Is that right? You have been talking about the possibility of marriage?"

Tom and Sam both nodded.

"You have not known each other for long. Have you prayed about this, Samantha?"

"Not about marriage specifically, but whether Tom is the man God has chosen for me. It seemed improbable since we live so far apart."

"What changed your mind?"

"The day I was leaving, everything felt wrong. Then when Tom showed up, it seemed right again. It's hard to explain. It was a really strong feeling."

"I had that feeling, too," Tom said. "I knew that if she left without me, I would regret it for the rest of my life."

"It sounds like God was talking to you both. My advice is to continue praying and getting to know each other. Communication is key, even long distance. Don't get impatient. If it is meant to be, it will be."

"Thank you, father."

"You're welcome, dear. I hope we will meet again, Tom."

Tom shook his hand. "Thank you, Father."

They walked out of the church hand in hand, and Sam asked, "Did talking to him help?"

"It helped a lot. Thank you. I feel like a weight has been lifted."

"Good. Let's go visit Tia's plant shop. I think you will like it. I always feel happy there."

They spent the rest of the morning looking around, then met Torque at the Ugly Orange Cafe. Sam never got tired of the bright orange tiles and greenhouse-style windows. Bringing a large group to town for shopping and lunch was a nice bonus for local businesses as well. Since there were so many of them, Sam had called ahead and asked for a large salad and a couple of lasagnas to take home for dinner.

While they were eating, Dani complained that everyone was staring.

Sam smiled at Dani, then looked at Cathy. "Do you remember when we first met?"

"I do, and I feel so lucky that we did."

"What I'm getting at is that we never know what is causing someone to stare. They might be staring because you are cool, fabulous, and confident. Or they might be staring because you are noisy, and they aren't used to that. Either way, don't assume. Be like Cathy and ask. She changed my life that day."

After lunch, they returned to the ranch, and everyone was told to make themselves at home and do whatever they liked. Sam spent some time talking to the ladies and took Tom for his first horse ride. Although she was going to miss the crazy group of misfits, Sam thought a little bit of peace and quiet might be nice. She smiled at herself. *Imagine that.*

The next morning, she waved goodbye to Torque and was left alone with Tom and Marcus. "Do you have three horses we can ride?" Tom asked. "I want to show you something."

"Sure. We can take Parsnip and Herbie."

"Herbie?" Marcus asked.

"The love bug." Sam smiled. "You can't help but love her."

"Good thing you have that magic closet."

"Wait," Tom said. "What magic closet?"

"Show him the magic," Sam told Marcus. "I'll have Roger get the horses ready."

Tom and Marcus exited the house looking like bonafide cowboys. They were smiling ear to ear and elbowing each other. Sam rolled her eyes comically, and Roger helped them up onto their saddles.

Sam didn't know it, but Roger had also helped Tom with directions, so he led the way. "Where are you taking us?" Sam asked.

"You'll see."

After about half an hour, Tom slowed and led them up to a large house. A man in jeans and a t-shirt came out of the house, followed by a sleepy-looking St. Bernard. Sam thought the man looked scarier than his dog. He was bald and muscular, and he was holding a rifle.

"Hello, Mr. Jimenez? I'm Tom. We spoke on the phone."

"Yes, I remember. Who is Sam?"

"This is Sam." Tom indicated. "Sam, Mr. Jimenez runs a survival school."

Sam's eyes got very round. "I can't believe it!" She jumped off Ghost and walked up to the man with her hand outstretched. "I'm so happy to meet you."

The St. Bernard began a low growl.

"Bear. Heel. You can call me Art." He shook Sam's hand. "Why don't we go inside and talk. Your friends can entertain Bear. Bear, you be good."

Once inside, Sam looked around. The decor was eclectic. It looked like a combination of a centuries-old mansion with the requisite family heirlooms and a hunting lodge with stuffed animal heads, rifles, and old maps.

"Have a seat. Your friend Tom told me a little bit about you. I don't often mentor new instructors, but I was intrigued."

They both sat in large stuffed chairs. *I wonder if I'll be able to get back out of this chair.*

"I saw that you rode here bareback. Do you do that often?"

201

"Ghost knows me. I never use a saddle or bridle with her unless I'm transporting gear."

"What kind of gear?"

"Usually camping stuff. Occasionally rock-climbing gear."

"Where do you usually camp?"

"In the mountains above my ranch."

"What kind of shelter do you use?"

"A tent or a tarp."

"And how do you cook?"

"Over a campfire."

"Do you take your own food?"

"Usually, but sometimes I forage or set traps."

And so, the questioning continued until Art decided that Sam had enough aptitude and experience to train with him.

"If you are serious about getting certified, we can train four days a week for six weeks or until you can pass the certification exam."

"That sounds amazing!"

"We can start on Monday. Is that okay with you?"

"Yes. Absolutely!"

"Great. Here is a list of things you should bring." He handed her a list. "Do you have any questions?"

"What time should I arrive?"

"How about six a.m.?"

Sam nodded. "Should I drive here?"

"Yes. We'll travel on foot from here."

"Thank you. I'm looking forward to it."

They went back outside to find Marcus rolling on the ground, laughing and fending off Bear's slobbery tongue. Art shook his head and strode over to Tom. He stuck his hand out and said, "Sam seems to have an amazing aptitude for survival training. Thank you for recommending her."

"You're welcome. I hope it works out." Tom looked over at Sam, smiling like it was Christmas, and his heart melted. Then he looked at Marcus, giggling like a child. "Ready to go, Marcus?"

"Yep." He gave Bear a shove. "Off you go, you giant, slobbery galoot!" Bear gave a giant leap and landed right on top of him, knocking the wind out of him.

"Bear! Heel!" Art said sternly. Bear looked a little sad as he left his new friend and went to stand by his owner.

"Bye, Bear." Marcus waved and went to mount Herbie.

"Want a leg up?" Sam asked.

"Yes, please."

"Me too," Tom said.

Sam mounted Ghost with a running leap, and they all waved at Art and Bear as they headed back to the ranch.

Sam was quiet on the way back, but once they had handed the horses off to Roger, she could no longer contain herself. Her excitement bubbled over, and she talked non-stop while she made dinner.

They ate and played games and sang karaoke. When they finally went to bed, Sam had trouble winding down until Tom's imminent departure hit her. She snuggled up next to him and said, "I don't want you to go."

"I know, but it will be okay. You work on your training, and we'll talk every day. We'll be together again before you know it." He held her close until he felt her relax into slumber, but his own eyes refused to close.

Morning came too soon, and Tom was exhausted. He watched Marcus bouncing around, excited to return to Las Vegas. Sam looked subdued as she started coffee, then breakfast.

She laughed when she saw him watching and said, "Don't judge. I have my priorities." He walked up behind her and put his arms around her waist. Nuzzling her neck, he whispered, "Cook slowly. I don't want to go."

She turned and gave him a kiss. "I don't want you to go either."

Marcus made a face. "Stop with all of this gooey stuff. You're ruining my appetite."

"Coffee is what *you* need, grouchy pants." She poured them each a cup and started the bacon. Tom sat back down at the table and talked to Marcus about their route. He looked up at Sam every once in a while and smiled. *I've gotten so used to seeing her every day. This is going to be hard.*

Sam watched Tom and Marcus as she finished making breakfast. They were an unlikely pair, but she could see a real friendship forming. *I hope they will stay friends. Tom needs more than just his work. And I hope Marcus will stay in touch.*

"Come and get it," she called, placing food on their plates. They both got up and took their breakfasts.

Marcus gave his a sniff. "Smells grreat!"

"Where's the silverware?" Tom asked.

Sam pointed to a drawer by the dishwasher.

Once they all got to the table and began to eat, Sam jumped up. "Shoot. I forgot the cinnamon rolls." She opened the oven and breathed a sigh of relief. "Whew. Not burned."

"Thank god," Marcus said. "I was going to die of disappointment if they were."

Sam's smile wobbled a little. "Will you visit again when Tom comes?".

"Of course! I'll bring Darren if he can get time off. Then we can fight gooey with gooey."

"Let us do the dishes, Sam. It's the least we can do after you cooked us this amazing breakfast." Tom stood with his plate.

"Okay. You do that while I pack you some travel snacks."

When they were ready to go, Sam hugged them both several times. She stood in the drive and waved as they drove onto the dusty road and away from the ranch. She felt sad but hopeful at the same time. *Tom is right. This time is different. It's the beginning of our story, not the end. I have so many things to look forward to.*

Alice Kanaka has been reading everything she could get her hands on since she could hold a book and writing stories aboutthe world around her. Her youth was a series of moves across the United States, accompanied by her sibling sidekick and her books.

After studying abroad in England and Spain and a short stint working for Club Med, Alice packed her bag once more and went to teach in Japan. Her story continues along the same vein, adding languages, kid sand cats into the mix. Open one of her mysteries to see the world through her eyes. You won't be disappointed.

HTTPS://AliceKanaka.com

If you'd like to see more of Alice's adventures, make sure to check out her **travel blog!**

https://ExploringWithAlice.com

Sign up for Alice's mailing list to get notifications and to be entered in a monthly raffle!

Coming Soon:
The Cardinal & the Hawk

Made in the USA
Middletown, DE
24 October 2022

13406858R00125